Almost Love

Kate Sparrows

Kate Sparrows; kate.sparrows@gmail.com
https://www.facebook.com/ksparrows

Publisher's Note: This is a work of fiction. Names, characters, places, and incidents are a product of the author's imagination. Locales and public names are sometimes used for atmospheric purposes. Any resemblance to actual people, living or dead, or to businesses, companies, events, institutions, or locales is completely coincidental.

Cover Design: Lorena Martin
Printed by CreateSpace, An Amazon.com Company

Almost Love/ Kate Sparrows. -- 1st ed.
ISBN 978-1-943797-14-1

"Be yourself; everyone else is already taken."

— Oscar Wilde

Chapter One

The bed springs were creaking loudly, probably waking her neighbors. But that wasn't going to stop what was going on in the bedroom. Cora knew pain, and she wasn't one to stop short. Each loud creak cheered her on and only stopped after she gave it one last hurrah. With the last bit of strength, the button on her jeans slid into the hole and it was over. The zipper gave in next. As she sat up, Cora remembered her explicit interactions with a footlong meatball sandwich, a chocolate milkshake, and a side order of French fries. Worst of all was her lethargic end to the night passed out on the futon. Now she was forced to deal with the slight digging in of fabric around her midsection for an entire day. But she smiled proudly in the mirror as she tried to tame the wild mess now atop her head. At least she managed to squeeze into the skinny jeans. That was enough of a victory for today.

Of course, it was more or less a day to herself, but there were still errands to run. After all the years of watching her mother calmly tend to four children, run a household and keep the finances straight, you'd think that Cora would have this under control. But at twenty-

She decided on a package of Italian sausage, thinking that pizza would be a wonderful way to celebrate joining the eating world again. Plus, it could last two days if she didn't inhale the whole meaty pie in one sitting. When she reached for a package, a voice spoke out.

"I see you like sausage."

She turned to see a hot guy looking at her. The dark-haired god was probably just under six feet tall and built like a steamy dream. Her best friend, Clarice, would probably wager that he had the sexy vee on his hips and a happy little treasure trail that led down to the biggest dick ever. Clarice would probably go on about the sexcapades and the trouble she could get into with this one. Cora just knew this was probably the corniest pick-up line she ever heard.

"Well, it is the best topping."

"Topping, huh?" The guy's lips pulled up into a smirk. Just the way he said it oozed sexual innuendoes. Cora hadn't caught on soon enough that she would be the pizza to his sausage topping on her. When she did, it kind of sucked. She had hoped that he was someone that wasn't just interested in her looks or had seen her doppelganger's pornos. But it also threw her mind in the gutter when she thought about what this guy might actually be able to do. "Is that an invitation?"

"Oh, god, no," Cora blurted. She didn't want him to think that she was just desperate woman that would jump anything.

His expression flipped and he just stared at her like she had three heads and was covered in neon feathers. Of course, she had three heads! He didn't look like the type to ever be turned down and, yet, Cora had. It was unthinkable. Then he busted his gut laughing.

"Good one. You had me going there." He reached out his hand. "Dylan Haggerty."

"Uh." This was definitely awkward. Cora wanted to slap away his hand for laughing at her, but it was just wounded feelings. It seemed like her chances were lost. And, seriously, when was the last time that a hot guy took interest in her? Shit. That was it. Cora stuck out her hand and shook his. "Cora Valencia."

"Pleasure." That sexy smile came back to his face and – the way he said it – Cora was sure that it could be. "How about you let me take you out for some pizza action?"

Guess guys nowadays were extra bold and stupidly blunt. Too bad she wasn't up for a tumble between the sheets with... toppings. Cora knew she wasn't one that really cared for one-night stands or even friends-with-benefits. That wasn't her kind of thing. Even in a relationship, it wasn't something she really needed – fantasized about, sure. Cora was still human. Even so, her ex-boyfriend only got as far as one pregnancy scare after "forgetting" to pull out to turn her off sex – and that had been with someone she trusted. That meant she wasn't too eager for Dylan to have a go.

"Forget the pizza," she started. He could probably forget any kind of sex plans he was thinking about. If he wanted that, he had to stick around and put in the work. "Ever play mini golf?"

Again, Dylan laughed. Seriously, did he think she was a joke? He didn't need to laugh at everything she said. It made her believe that her ex-boyfriend may have really been onto something when she stopped fooling around with him. All those things he had said and called her those years ago where creeping back into her thoughts. There had to be a reason no other man showed interest, and it wasn't just because she was a fashion whore and half broke. Her curvy size 14 hips and five-foot stature must have had something to do with it. She wasn't the thin, pretty, athletic blonde that guys like Dylan dated.

"You are just a bundle of surprises, huh?" He was gently shaking his head, but there was a mischievous smile on his face. Before Cora could figure out what he meant, much less get a chance to ask, he said that he's never been. And somehow, it was decided that it would be a date. "Sure. Thursday night. I'll meet you at Cubbie's Putt Putts."

He reached for her hand, giving it a little squeeze. It sent a tingle along her skin. Why was he affecting her so much? Dylan was just a cocky stranger. Pulling a pen from his back pocket, he scribbled down seven digits on her palm. "Text me so I can get your digits."

So, there was still a way out of this, if she came to her senses. Dylan had been so sure, so cocky. There was always that slim chance that he actually like her for her and because not taking the chance was a guarantee that nothing would happen. Or she could walk away, finish her shopping, and forget his sexy smile and that laugh. Besides, she was pretty sure that he was lying right now. If he never played mini golf then how did he know the name of the only putt-putt course in the city? He definitely didn't seem the type that played that sport.

Unfortunately, it was one of the very few sports that Cora could play without looking like a fool or a wildebeest shoved into a too-tight sport uniform.

Cora watched – still slightly shocked – as he picked up a package of chicken wings and headed towards the registers. She wasn't entirely sure what to make of him and the interaction. Looking down at the phone number on her hand, she wondered if this was a fake number or one for those automatic answering machines. Would it insult her or turn her down or sign her up for a hundred daily email spam newsletters? Maybe – like, if she really was going to consider texting Dylan – she could use a reverse phone number lookup online. That would rule out an automated hotline number, at least.

She headed towards the registers but stopped halfway there when she realized that she actually hadn't put the sausage in her basket. Dylan had thrown her off when she grabbed it and she had ended up setting it back down. Rolling her eyes at her own stupidity, Cora headed back to grab the meat before getting in line at the register.

These register girls had it the roughest. They had to deal with all kinds of bullshit and, probably, had more guys hitting on them here for discounts on their supersized bag of Doritos and Mountain Dew instead of clipping coupons in their gaming dens. Cora couldn't really relate at her job, seeing as she worked in a department store where it was mostly women buying horrible mass-produced crap. She did know how ridiculous it was to watch – helpless – as unready people fumbled with their wallets and then struggle over the concept of taking their bags of over-priced goodies. What was worse was being the person in line behind that person and being unable to carry out your plans of murdering that person because you still wouldn't get through the register any faster.

She made sure that everything was emptied out on the conveyor belt by the time it was her turn. It wasn't a huge haul, but it would get her through another week without breaking the bank. Besides, that would leave more money for clothes and other pretty things later. Cora could always hit up the online stores, especially after she knew that she wouldn't have to worry about eating and living somewhere first. If things got desperate, there was always the option for a visit home. It was a last resort, but it would save Cora from starving. Her family was a lot to handle. Then again, starving didn't sound like such a bad way to go after all...

"That'll be ten fifty," the cashier said.

Cora had to shake herself out of her thoughts to avoid being the thing she hated. She apologized – just in case she had been zoned out for longer than she thought – and coughed up the cash. It was hard to hand over that much, especially when she realized that she basically picked up enough food to make a pizza and breakfast tomorrow. Hitting up Subway for a footlong would have cost her less.

She grabbed the bags and the little bit of change before making her way back into the brisk Boston air. It seemed like the city had woken up now. Buses and car horns went off every few minutes now. Bicyclists and runners were zooming around. Tons of suitcase-toting beings flooded the sidewalks. Everything was in full force. All Cora wanted to do was make it home and get away from people today.

Then there was the question of what to do with Dylan's number. All the groceries had been put away and now the post-it note kept turning over in her hands. Cora had written it down when she got home so that it wouldn't smudge or wash off, but now she wasn't sure if she wanted it. It left the temptation and chance of setting herself up for humiliation. Would he laugh at her if she texted him? Would he be laughing because he was so far out of her league and she stupidly fell for it?

Dylan could be a guy out of one of those romance books, if all this was real. He certainly came off as over the top and he definitely played with the sexual innuendoes instead of coming right out to say what he wanted. Saying "toppings" had let her mind wander to all the ways that they could get after each other and all the different positions in different places around her apartment – or her imaginary version of his apartment – to do it. It made for a good fantasy but maybe it wouldn't be the best in real life. It wasn't like she had gone looking for this, but there was the opportunity. And why not take it? Dylan was definitely a couple steps up from her ex-boyfriend.

It was just seven numbers though. One guy. It wasn't like she had anything else going on, especially on a Thursday night. And who picked Thursday night of all times? It wasn't the weekend where everyone else would be out on dates because people weren't working. It wasn't the Friday date night that could easily carry over to the next day, like Saturday could. It wasn't Monday where it would be the "great start" to the week and where you could easily set up a second date for that coming weekend. Thursday night was like the day to go out when you didn't want to run into anyone else – almost like a shame date. It definitely was too close to the weekend to allow the standard time between dates, so it was a whole week that Cora would have to wait if this was a legit thing that went well.

Mini golf was harmless. It was just nine holes to go and shoot the breeze over, trying to do small talk. If the guy wanted to waste his time with her, then why not take advantage of that? If nothing else, she could prove to her ex-boyfriends wrong – she *was* interesting. That decided it. There were more pros than cons, and this didn't need to be a long-term thing to be worth it. Cora could always bring up this date when her family questioned her about her dating life. If they knew she went on a date, it might take some of the heat off. For all she knew, her family thought that she was refusing to date, staying at home, being a slob, and adopting a hundred cats that would eventually eat her soul and body.

Hi, it's Cora.

It was a simple text, but that's really all she could have done. If she pushed and asked how his day was or how he was doing, it might sound too nosy or pushy. She didn't know anything else about him to start a real conversation. He had picked up chicken wings at the grocery store, but that didn't mean that he made them for dinner. Otherwise, it would have been perfectly acceptable to bring up food and ask how the wings turned out.

Staring at the cell phone's screen, she half-expected a text back instantly. After how forward Dylan had been, she thought that he wouldn't have waited a second to type back a witty message. Then again, it was proving a little that she might have been the joke after all.

But why hadn't he texted her back yet? It had already been three minutes.

Cora set down the phone and decided that she needed to do something more productive... like clean her apartment. She had gone to the kitchen to grab the foaming cleaner and was halfway to the bathroom when she decided better – and more realistically. She was not that desperate to resort to cleaning when she could just do some retail therapy online or, really, anything else. Like actually make the pizza that she was going to make. With all the debate over Dylan's number, it had slipped to the back of her thoughts.

The dough was easy enough to make – just add water to the packaged mix and stretch out on a pan. The sausage needed to be browned and broken up before it could make it on the pizza. Halfway through making the pizza, Cora was still distracted and glancing at her phone for text messages. If she was going to keep her sanity then she was going to need a better distraction that cooking, and the pizza was already assembled now. What would really go well with pizza would be a movie... a free one.

Armed with her library card, she ventured out again. It wasn't far away but it meant that she needed to bundle up again. She strolled along the solemn rows of ancient texts and media devices. Books from early 2000s and VHS tapes with low-quality special effects were filling the shelves that rose up on either side of her. There was only a small selection of titles that would play on her old – yet modern – disc reading device. It looked like there was a few more movie titles added since her last binge. Her favorite was checked in, but not for long. Cora grabbed *Pride & Prejudice*. She loved herself a bit of Mr. Darcy and that old moxie that ladies were missing nowadays. If it wasn't for the horribly uncomfortable looking clothing, Cora would have found a way to go back in time and marry the man herself after Elizabeth foolishly sent him off.

Silently, she made her way to the check-out line. Unlike the ones she suffered through at work and the grocery store, this one was very short, and it made sense because libraries were one of those places that people always overlooked. The benefit was that Cora didn't need to deal with a ton of people. The librarian asked for her card and the movie, scanned them, then handed them back. Mr. Darcy was now hers for a week! How could people not use libraries more? Have a return? Just drop it in the bin by the door. It was a simple process and the best part – silence. You didn't have to talk to anyone, and the library was always nice and quiet. No snarky comments or flirty banter. It would be nice if Cora only had to deal with this. She would probably love her job too much and never leave.

Cora took her movie and headed home. As much as she hated to admit it, that phone stole her mind and soul. It had her by the purse-strings… heart-strings. It was impossible not to check to see if Dylan texted back. It had been almost an hour. And nothing. She threw the pizza into the oven to cook and slide the movie into the DVD player. Pacing the floor of the apartment, Cora tried to talk herself out of texting him again. Maybe he didn't see her first message. A second message he would definitely see. Maybe mini golf wasn't really his thing. She could suggest something else. Or maybe this really was all just a sick joke to get her hopes up to crash them in some kind of power trip. Well, that was it. She wasn't going to let him have any more control over her emotions. She was going to block his number and forget him over Mr. Darcy and some hot, steamy, --*Ding!*

She had a text!

Hey bby! U Xcited? I am.

"Oh, my god! Oh, my god!" Cora bounced as she read the text again. He was excited for their date! She squealed and tried to think of something great to text him back. Nothing was coming to mind. She was just so excited that he texted back at all. Nothing that came to her mind sounded as good as what he wrote. She couldn't text back and sound like an idiot not.

Yea. It's gonna be fun!

Okay. That wasn't the best thing ever to text back, but it was something. Dylan wouldn't think that she was ignoring him, but he might be thinking that she was desperately waiting by the phone for him to text her. It hadn't even taken her a minute to text back. Cora groaned as she plopped down on the couch and used her arms to cover her face. She messed it all up again.

Who was she trying to kid? She was a bit desperate. Cora wanted his guy to talk to her. She wanted him to want her. It wasn't like he was the The One but she didn't want to be alone forever; and, while Dylan was a terrible flirt, she thought there might be something there. Of course, underneath all that talk, there was a chance that they'd have things in common and get along great. If not, there was the whole experience of dating. It was worth the chance.

She had to make the move and show him that she really was interested. Cora hadn't expected to be interested at all and now he was under her skin. He probably didn't walk into that grocery store and talk to her expecting that she would be interested. Maybe she needed to change his thoughts about that and let him know that she was interested in knowing him.

I can't stop thinking about you.

More or less because she wondered if he'd text her back again or not. Hopefully he hadn't just texted her back and now she was off his radar until Thursday. That wasn't the case though. It seemed like it had been the right thing to do when Dylan texted back an emoji smiley face. Maybe he had been thinking about her too.

Chapter Two

Clothes went flying everywhere. Cora groaned as more things went flying out of the closet, over her head. This wasn't good enough for Dylan. Nothing seemed like a good enough outfit for their date. She had to try harder, find a cuter outfit, find something more put together. She dove deeper into the closet. In the back, she managed to find something that wasn't a complete train wreck. Turns out it was no easy task to put a matching outfit together when most of her closet was tossed off the hangers all over her room. Maybe she was just a tad over the top with this. It was just an outfit for a mediocre date with a guy that she wasn't exactly into. It wasn't like he was someone that she really wanted to spend the rest of her life with. There was no need to get unreasonably attached to Dylan at this point in their relationship. That was too absurd. There was no relationship yet and no reason to put that much pressure on herself, and for no reason at all. She might as well focus that hardship on her waist size. A couple sizes smaller wouldn't kill her chance and maybe if she slipped down a few sizes then she could really get a guy like Dylan.

Cora settled on a pair of dark skinny wash jeans and a white baby doll tunic. She grabbed a jean jacket to throw on top, just in case the weather wanted to get a little windy or there's a chill outside. The weather app on her phone said it was going to be warm and sunny all day. It was safe to say that she could trust the weather app today because, when she hurried to catch the bus, it was that perfect kind of day.

The bus was a little crowded, but nothing could dampen her day. Not when she felt cute in her outfit and excited for meeting up with Dylan. The bus stop was just a couple blocks away now. It barely felt like it took any time at all to get here. She crossed the street and headed into the putt-putt ticket office, expecting to see Dylan already there with a putter in each hand. When she walked in, that wasn't what she saw. There were just a couple people lingering around and only a couple were out on the course putting.

She checked her phone – no texts from Dylan. It was the time that they were supposed to meet. It would have been nice if he had said if he was running late or had to reschedule. She checked the time again, debating how long to wait before calling it quits and going home with a carton of ice cream to wallow. This had been a mistake.

"Hey, sorry I'm late. I walked out of the wrong subway exit and then traffic got in the way." Dylan beamed a smile and it kind of made her forget that he was late. There was really no harm done.

"It's alright. You're here now." Best not to hold onto what could have been and just enjoy what was happening. If she held onto the doubts that had crept in, then she wouldn't actually be in the present with Dylan. If she didn't, then it definitely would mess things up.

"Okay, so just wait here and I'll get us tickets." He started to walk away. "What color ball do you want?"

"Purple." Cora then thought to add, "It's my favorite color."

"Okay."

Dylan just left it at that. She watched him pay and get everything. He just picked a normal white golf ball. Unlike her, he hadn't reciprocated with his favorite color and his choice in ball didn't really say anything either. There was a chance that he liked white, but probably not. Favorite colors didn't really matter anyways. There were plenty of other more important things to learn about each other and maybe that's what Dylan was going to focus on instead.

"I'll keep track of the score. That is if you can try me not to cheat." He winked while he handed over a putter and the purple golf ball.

"Naw, I trust you." It also meant that Cora wouldn't have to worry about doing math, which seemed like a lot more work. If he was willing to do that, then she wasn't going to stop him.

"Well, then, ladies first." He held out his arm and let her head to the first hole.

Cora leaned down and set her ball behind the line on the AstroTurf. Standing up, she glanced back at Dylan to see a smirk on his face. She turned away quick, feeling her own face heat up. He was so checking out her ass, and she could only hope that these skinny jeans had made it look good. Then again, judging by that smirk, they had. She wasn't entirely sure how she felt knowing that he once again was focused on her looks.

She lined up her shot and gave the ball a gentle tap to get it near the first hole. The slight hill towards the back stopped her ball from rolling right off the course, but also made it stop a couple feet shy.

"Not bad," Dylan commented.

He stepped up to place his ball. In no way did he hide the fact that he wanted Cora to check him out. Not that she hadn't thought about doing just that. Clarice would ever let her live it down if she couldn't tell her what Dylan's ass looked like. And, from what she saw, it was a decent one. It wasn't flat nor was it a badonkadonk. The rest of the details she could just make up if Clarice questioned her.

"Wow, lucky shot." Cora watched his putt go all the way to the hole.

He laughed. "Yep, I believe they call that a hole-in-one."

A hole-in-one it was. It seemed a little odd that he sank that putt on the first try. Dylan didn't even need her to tell him how to set up the ball or how to read the hole. He did see her go first and maybe that was enough. He had placed his ball exactly where she had placed her. He must have seen that she didn't quite hit it hard enough. Plus, the first hole was always the easiest. There were no tiny ponds or wood blocks in the way. If Dylan was lucky enough to get a hole-in-one, it should be on the first hole.

Cora walked up to her ball and tapped it in. Calling out her two strokes, he wrote down the score and they moved on to the second hole. Cora knew this one was trickier. There was a tiny water hazard on the side of the green, which would have been the perfect angle to get to the hole. May times it had captured Cora's ball, and this time was no different. The purple ball splashed into the water, causing her to take a mulligan. But by some beginner's luck, Dylan got around it. Within three putts, his ball was in the hole.

"You're really good at this," she commented.

He just shrugged it off. "Well, I'm good at a lot of things."

"I'd bet," she mumbled under her breath. But judging from the smirk on his face, Dylan had heard that.

"I could show you later," he offered.

The pizza came back to her mind. Yea, that was probably one of those things. She wasn't sure that she wanted to see anything right now. She would rather get to know more about this random guy that flirted with her in a grocery store. Like, there had to be a better story there.

"You could just tell me," she tried. Maybe if he listed some things then she would know the kind of stuff he was into and what his skills were. Cora was willing to bet that maybe he was an athlete in high school or had played real golf before, but never putt-putt.

"Naw." He shook his head. "It's better if I show you."

That was disappointing, to say the least. It was like he was a closed book – unless it was flirting. She watched him struggle with the wooden blocks on the next hole while she sailed straight on through – having mastered the right angles over the years. For being a date, there wasn't a whole lot of talking and getting to know each other. It was rather odd. It felt like they were just dancing around each other and dancing around the idea of figuring the other person out.

Cora was getting to the point where it was starting to bother her. Was this really a date or what the hell was this? Maybe – for all this cocky talk – he needed her to make the first move. "So, what do you like to do for fun, Dylan?"

"Um, well," he shrugged, "this, I guess."

"You don't know?" Oh, she wasn't going to let him get away without talking about himself and giving her a real answer. "So, what would you be doing if you weren't here with me?"

Dylan stopped, mid-putt, and straightened up his posture. "Huh, that's a good question. I'm not really sure."

Yea, not really sure her ass. Cora would bet that if he wasn't here with her then he'd be out on a date with someone else. It didn't give her a good feeling to imagine that. That was the thing that she hated about the dating game. You go out to try and invest your time with a person and they're off investing their time with someone else. Then they never end up picking you in the end so it's all just a waste of time.

"Well, do you like sports or do you like working on cars?" Although, it didn't look like he used his hands for any hard or physical labor.

He shook his head. "Naw, best to leave cars to the professionals."

"So, sports? Like did you play any or you a fan of the Red Sox?" It really shouldn't be this hard.

"Are you trying to get to know me?" He asked, putting a hand on his hip.

Well, duh. Cora just nodded.

"Okay, so I'm not a fan of sports but my family is big Patriots fans. I played soccer and basketball in high school but didn't do well enough to get a scholarship for college. I am naturally talented with anything physical. I don't touch cars because I wouldn't want to be the reason a simple problem turns into totaling my car, and I also don't have a car to touch."

Wow, that was the most that he ever spoke about himself. It really wasn't much to think about in terms of who he was as a person, but it definitely was something. Cora wasn't a sports fan, so they at least matched in that regard. She didn't have a car either, but her reason was more because she couldn't afford it. She was willing to bet that Dylan didn't have one because the public transit system in Boston was fairly good.

"Is there anything else you want to know?" He asked, but it was like more out of obligation and not out of genuine sharing.

Cora didn't want to scream *"Yes!"* because there was a lot she wanted to know. There was a lot more that she would expect to know before starting a real relationship with Dylan. There were just somethings you needed to know – like are they vegan or smoker? There were lifestyle choices that could clash, and it was better to find that out before getting too deep. Although, those chicken wings he picked up ruled out him being vegan or vegetarian and, in all the time they spent out here putting, he hadn't lit a cigarette. She now knew that he

30

graduated high school and went off to college, so he wasn't as dumb as he played.

Taking a page out of his book, she shrugged. "Guess I know all I need to for now."

Dylan turned back to take his shot, finishing up the round. He headed towards a bench and Cora followed, taking a seat next to him. She watched as he tallied up their scores. She hadn't done too bad – making par on the course, even with the distraction of Dylan. Dylan on the other hand was a couple strokes under par, meaning that he won.

"Looks like you won," Cora pointed out.

"Looks like I did." He laughed and his smile grew. "So, what's my reward?"

She stared at him in disbelief. "Um, I didn't know we were playing for something."

"Would you have tried harder?" He asked.

"I tried the normal amount." She tried not to take that as an offensive stab. "Well, I don't know what to give you as a reward. Um, you could have bragging rights?"

"Naw, I already got those." He shook his head slightly. "How about you give me another date?"

Cora wasn't sure if he was being real or not. She had been set on this date being a fluke or a horrible joke. She was walking away from it not really knowing much about Dylan, and he hadn't asked anything about her. One date could be a fluke and written off as a good story to tell, but a second date meant that this thing could be more serious.

What would Clarice do?

Clarice would jump this guy. That's what she would do. Cora could recognize what a catch he was, even if he wasn't really opening up at all. He was out of her league, but being with him would bring her up a level or two. And what did she really have to lose?

"Okay, but I'm not sure how that's a reward."

He reached over and took her hand. "Oh, it's a reward to me."

"So, what do you want to do?" Cora almost regretted wording it that way when he smirked, but there was no other way to say it. "And like what day works for you?"

Dylan held out his hand for her putter, which she handed over along with the golf ball. "Well, the second date is going to be a secret for now."

"Meaning you have no idea, right?"

He laughed. "See? You know me already."

Okay, so he hadn't really thought it out either. Maybe he was pleasantly surprised by Cora and how things went just like she was. Or maybe he was more of the spontaneous type. After all, it had been Cora who suggested mini golf as a date.

"Alright, so then do you know when you want to go out? I'm just asking in case I need to take off from work." Luckily, she didn't have to for this date.

"Oh, where do you work?"

It was the first personal question that he asked her, but she wasn't so sure that she wanted to be too precise in her answer. "A department store out in Back Bay."

"Cool." Although, he didn't seem that impressed. Honestly, working as a cashier wasn't that impressive, so he was right on thinking that. "Well, how about you text me what days you're off and we'll plan it out later?"

"Okay." Cora got up and followed him to the equipment return. It did feel like he was kind of rushing the date to be over. If he wanted this to be over and get rid of her, why bother to bring up a second date? It was just confusing, and she was sure that Clarice would have something to say about it later.

Dylan stuck his hands in his pocket as they left. He was probably going to take a left and head to the subway while she was going to take a right and walk a bit to get to the bus stop. They had a plan, but this was it. They would go their own way, but Cora didn't know how this date would end. With his hands in his pocket, there probably wouldn't be a goodbye hug or – shudder – a handshake. She wasn't so sure that a kiss would be appropriate either.

"So, I guess I'll see you around?" She asked, hoping to clue him into how awkward this goodbye was. She was also hoping that he would decide on how they said goodbye.

"Yea. I'll catch ya later."

She watched for a moment as he walked away. Cora expected him to stop and glance back at her or to come walking back to steal that kiss. That's what would have happened in all the romance novels and movies. Mr. Darcy wouldn't have just walked away and left Elizabeth like this. One thing was for sure – Dylan wasn't a Darcy.

Chapter Three

Dylan had been a little ridiculous on the golf course the other day – claiming not to play mini golf and then navigating through the clown faces and windmills with ease. He had won and maybe it was just to impress her that this beginner could play well. Then again, he might have only won because he was a stubborn distraction. Cora had caught him checking her out multiple times and then he seemed to dodge almost every attempt she made to get to know him. She had focused on the date aspect of things while he had been focusing on winning – or impressing her. With Dylan, she wasn't sure what that cocky smirk's intention truly was.

Then there was the fact that the date wasn't even over yet before he asked for another one. It definitely was unexpected, but it also was a letdown. He hadn't planned it out with her then and promised to talk to her later about it. So far, Dylan had been MIA. It was that temptation dangling like a Gucci bag in front of her, but it was tied to a string that was tied to a stick that was attached to her back – keeping it just out of reach. She had to re-watch *Pride & Prejudice* for a fourth time after grabbing a pint of ice cream from the corner bodega. Her thighs were not going to thank her. To add insult to injury, it was now Tuesday.

Tuesday mornings were always such a drag. It was the only day that she religiously worked because her boss was a bitch that way and needed to make herself free to shop all the sales at the other big stores. While it didn't seem like that helped Cora any, it gave her a whole shift without having to be lectured about smiling and volunteered for extra work around the store. Occasionally, she had been able to play this card to get days off with short notice. There was no way the boss was going to risk losing a dedicated grunt. That would mean no sales for her, which probably would just turn her into a bigger bitch and drive all the other employees away until the store closed. Then again, the Plastics were probably fine with a bitchy attitude. After all, they themselves were bitches.

Her phone went off as she climbed onto the bus. "Hello?"

"Hey." She'd recognize that voice. "I've been meaning to call."

Yea, meaning to call but never did. Cora waited a moment for an apology, but it looked like that was never coming. So, instead of keeping the awkward silence, she conversed like a semi-normal human being. "So, what's up?"

"Well, you owe me a second date. How about I pick you up and we get Thai?"

"Thai... like in the food?"

Dylan laughed. "Of course, like in the food. Unless you're into a threesome with random Asians."

That she was not. "Well, I've never had Thai food."

"What?" The shock was evident in his voice. "Everyone's had Thai food. I can't believe that."

There was a lot of things about Cora that he wouldn't believe. Chinese food was as exotic as she got. Well, minus the family gatherings were the tables were overflowing with the delicious Latin favorites and flavors. Just thinking about Vero Mango Paleta Con Chili made her mouth water. Those had the amazing spice of chili peppers in the center of the sweet mango sucker.

"Well, believe it. There's a lot I haven't had."

"I bet," he teased.

"Well, is it anything like General Tso?"

Dylan groaned on the other end. "No girl of mine is getting away with not knowing what Thai food is. Thursday you're coming over and I'm cooking."

Butterflies stormed her insides. Had Dylan really just called her *his girl*? Sure, it was far too soon to make such big implications about their relationship and slap labels on them. They'd only had one date, but maybe Dylan just knew. Maybe he knew that she was the one for him. Who was Cora to deny that? He was sexy and not completely full of shit. He was making her feel special just by talking to her like they were in the same league, and it was totally like all the fairytales said. She just had to relax and let it happen.

That was why she didn't bother to correct him on either assuming that she was free Thursday or about wanting to see him again or about being called his girl. It

37

was maybe obvious that she did want to see him again. Cora did pick up the phone and kept the conversation going, and maybe he saw it a little as flirting back. And who was she to kid? It was her day off, and even if it wasn't, she would have called in sick or swapped days with someone else just to make it work. Besides, free food. It was totally worth it with the constant threat of ramen nights.

"Just don't burn it," she teased, hoping that she came off smooth and jokingly.

He laughed and it set those butterflies in a tizzy again. "Babe, I don't burn things... but I do make things hot."

There was no doubt in her mind that he could make things very hot. But it was only going to be their second date and they hadn't even gotten on the subject of sex yet. So, all this flirting just seemed too soon. And it wasn't as if Cora was particularly looking forward to that subject either – the talk or the activity. She didn't want to be a pump-and-dump. It was just something that they needed to talk about first and someone needed to bring it up, even if it was going to derail the Dylan Train. It definitely cooled the rails every time she told a guy that she just wasn't into that... stuff. Guess when your doppelganger is a pornstar, not much else mattered.

"Hey, watching a hot guy cook is something that I can't miss." Hopefully that came off as cool and confident as Dylan had sounded.

Again, that sexy laugh filled the phone. "I'll see you Thursday then, babe."

He hung up and Cora couldn't help but feel like she was really over her head with this one. The guy was out of her league and his dating game was lightyears ahead of hers. At least Clarice had said they'd look hot together when she messaged her friend a secret photo she took when Dylan had been distracted by putting. Cora hadn't meant for it, but it turned out to be a great photo of his ass too. She had managed to get a better one of his face when he turned around to let her know it was her turn to tee off and had to play it as she was texting her sister – not photographing him. Well, Clarice was basically a sister but one that she actually picked and not like her real one. Actually, now that Cora thought about it, it was odd that her family was being rather quiet on the texting front. Usually there was one crisis or another going on in the Valencia household or, Cora shuddered, maybe her abuela was in town visiting.

That was one person that could derail all modern amenities and crack anyone back into form. One time, Cora had straightened her hair for school. Her abuela had blown a gasket over how she was trying to change who she culturally was and how their family was now going to suffer in shame; how their relatives were turning in their graves and going to seek them out on Dia de Muertos. No doubt her cellphone and microwave were going to be on her abuela's banned list. Great, just what she wanted for her date with Dylan – to show up smelling of smoke because they had to cook over the fire pit and how she smelled like pigeon – because that was going to be the only way Cora would be able to get a message out. Then again, were carrier pigeons even a legit thing anymore?

Or, maybe beyond all hope, Grandma Mariza forgot where she lived or that she was even part of the family. Yea, right. Hell would literally have to freeze over and Grandma Mariza would still somehow remember. She'd pull out the ancient family bible and somewhere around the end of the Old Testament would be her name, after the long list of every single member of their family. After that would be penciled in the approved names that she could give her unborn – and un-thought of – children. All of which were cycled and recycled in her family tree and voted on for each Valencia girl by their great-great-great old rotten relatives at some crazy bingo night. What Cora wouldn't give to crash that raging shindig and toss in a Maxwell or Mohamad or Arthur, just to mess with the old croons. No, she was stuck with Mateo, Santiago, Jorge, and Eduardo for any male heir that would come rushing out of her. Salomé and Ivanna were just not going to happen like Constanza.

Then again, Cora wasn't thinking about children at all so this really shouldn't bother her as much. She was pretty sure the whole sex thing still played a role in how those little demons were made. It helped that she hadn't the chance to do any of that. Plus, in her one bedroom flat, there was no room, or money, in her life for a baby. Luckily men weren't too interested in her curves either. Well, other than Dylan. And besides, he'd understand the whole not wanting to have sex and, or, kids part. There'd be fun date nights and flirting. Cuddling on the couch while watching something on Netflix was a hundred times better than some mattress mambo.

She tucked away her phone and thoughts as she got off the bus and headed into work. It was going to be another long day with annoyingly stupid people again. Cora tried to pull back her dark curly hair into a stylish bun, only to fail with a sloppy bun that got yanked out into a ponytail. She walked by the breakroom and quickly punched in before the minute hand on the clock passed. Once punched in, she took her time walking over to her register and flipping on the check-out lane's light to signal that she was "open for business". All around her were blondes with single digit waists and pink bubblegum-popping lips. Cora had tried to use the nail design appliques to get that French manicure look but these girls actually had one – and done by some uppity French nail artist too, no doubt. Her clothes were from right here at Lo-Mart while everyone else was sporting designer. One thing that she had going for her, though, was that all her clothing tags were in English. It was like the rest of her family who needed to prove they were Mexican by showing the whole world by their clothes and acting like that was the only way to be accepted. Cora could be Mexican and still be herself. Unlike her family and the shoppers in this store.

Cora wasn't sure why these girls bothered to come here when they could afford so much better fashion. Maybe it was to flaunt what they had and get a power trip off being better than everyone else in the whole store. One lady – who looked like she had way too much money to need to shop here – got into her line and started to fill up the conveyor belt. Cora tried to stay friendly with a smile but, really, what was the point? It wasn't like the cashiers got tipped for their service like waitresses, and this lady didn't come here to see her, personally. But god – if that were true – she'd totally be the perfect cashier, complete with handing out massages to every stressed lady to come through her line if they tipped her enough. No, she just had to deal with people like this woman and her Coach bag. This season's bag too! It wasn't even like it was last season's or a few years old that she bought on a sale rack or got secondhand off the internet. This gorgeous bag could only be a couple days old.

When the woman opened up her wallet to pay, Cora thought she was going to be locked up for murder. The woman didn't go for the platinum credit card just glistening there. It wasn't for the couple hundred-dollar bills that peeked out either. No, it was for the coupons that put her a condom's thickness away from raping the store. The plastic shopping bags cost more than what this woman was going to pay after all these coupons got rung up. It was mere pennies and when Cora handed back the woman's change, she giggled – *giggled* – when she dropped the coins into the Couch bag and grabbed her things to make an escape.

Something was rotten in the state of Demark and people like that pissed her off. The universe could take all Cora's money and sex drive, but it should have to give her something in return. Right? Law of conservation or some shit, right? That woman was living the life that Cora wanted, deserved. And how did she end up living in luxury? Just the luck of the draw or a corset for a tiny waist or turning into a salad-eating rabbit.

Cora didn't care that she was barely an hour into her shift. She flipped off the light before another entitled rich woman would rain on her day even more. She could just hide out in the breakroom and let the "Plastic" cashier girls handle their own kind for a while. They'd probably just chat for hours about how much better than everyone else they were and how it was a noble thing to volunteer to work in such an underprivileged place – really, those fake girls were the true heroes.

Uh, god!

She plopped down at the table in the breakroom and pulled out her cellphone. She knew Clarice was always up to hear the unreal stuff she had to put up with. If nothing else, she got to be catty about the idiots that graced her day. Of course, there was always the suggestion that Cora get a different job, one where she might be happier. The problem was that there was no job that was going to make her happy, unless there was some way magical way to do nothing, shop, and still get money in the bank. There was always the "marry a billionaire" option, but there were hardly any hot billionaires in the greater Boston area. Trust her. She looked. Clarice had gotten her to sign up for some bogus dating website, which really was just a cheap and cheesy site designed for hooking up. She had spent the better part of a weekend scouring the pages of profiles for anyone that didn't immediately turn her off – money or not – but hotties there were not. Dylan never popped up on that website, but she couldn't really see him being the type that would need to do the online dating thing. That kind of made what was happening between them a little more special and real. There was no algorithm saying they could hold a conversation or were a perfect match. There was no dating profile to ask stupid questions because they could ask each other those stupid question in their real conversations.

There wasn't a response right away from the "hey" text, which meant that her friend was in the middle of slinging sub sandwiches across town. Maybe it was worth getting a different job if she got to work with her best friend. It was only one bus stop away, and that was always Clarice's selling point to get her to convert. They both would be stuck with minimum wage jobs; and if Cora already hated ringing up rich women's purchases, getting her hands elbow-deep in their dressing-soaked sandwiches would be a living hell. Then again, work probably wouldn't happen at all if they were on the same shift. They'd probably spent the whole time gossiping and trying to out-do the other with the funniest memes, and they'd both get fired.

She was on her own for now. Groaning, Cora dropped her head on the table. All this bullshit at work was just putting her in a worse mood without a meme or joke from Clarice to pull her out of it. Really, she should be trying to focus on the good things going for her – like the impeding dinner date with her new hot boyfriend. But that was a confusing mess that she needed to talk to her friend about. It wasn't something to tackle alone. Okay, and maybe thinking of Dylan as her boyfriend already was a little too soon, but she needed some hope and something positive to cling onto right now. It definitely seemed like that's where Dylan's mind was anyways. He *did* just call her "his girl". Guys just don't claim girls like that if they don't actually want them.

The door creaked open and slammed shut. Turning her head to the side, Cora stared in horror as one of the plastic, fake girls came into the breakroom and sat down on the other side. She was already deep into her phone, texting or looking up a make-up tutorial or something. It didn't seem like Cora had been spotted yet, but she had a feeling that if she had been seen that nothing would have changed. To everyone else, she didn't exist. There was no way those plastic girls would ever talk to her, other than to try and get Cora to cover a shift so they could get a day off to be pampered at some spa or something equally ridiculous. Maybe she could make it out of this alive and with her days off still intact.

Cora got up and tried to quietly sneak around the far side of the room to stay out of the plastic girl's line of sight. She managed to slide along the tiled floor and make it to the ancient creaking door, which was surely going to expose this stealth mission. The longer that Cora paused here though, the greater the chances of being caught by this plastic girl or one of the others coming in for a break. She had to go now!

She darted out and was halfway back to her register when she dared to glance back over her shoulder. There was no one running her down, no one waving after her to stop. There wasn't even the rustle of t-shirts from the artificial air being pumped through the vents. Plastic girl hadn't even noticed her leave and didn't even hear the loud door. No one bothered to see Cora. Even the ancient door probably forgot her existence already. What did that say about her? The only people that cared if she existed or not were the line of superficial customers, all hungrily looking and waiting for her to turn on her register's light again.

Cora was doomed.

Grandma Mariza was in town.

Just as Cora's shift was ending and the freedom of those front sliding doors were in sight, her sister called and crushed her hopes of digging through her couch for change to buy more ice cream and veg out on her bed watching old telenovelas all night. It would have been easy to bail if it was just her sister asking to hang out or calling with the normal family dinner invite. But this wasn't at the request – demand rather – of their mother. Their mother, who just so happened to be on speaker phone with them. Their mother who just so happened to hear Cora pause too long and then try to weasel her way out of coming over for dinner with abuela. Their mother ended up taking her sister's phone away to lecture her for the whole bus ride back to Cora's apartment. She heard of all the ways that she was failing the family. It was just easier to give in and hide somewhere in her parent's house. With how many of them would actually be crammed into the small house, it surely wasn't going to be some small feat.

She headed up to her apartment and tried not to plan her grand escape to make a run for the border. Canada should have known it was only a matter of time before their borders were to be bombarded. They were too welcoming and nice of a country, even if it turned out to only be an untrue stereotype – it was still worth a try. If there ever was a plague of Latina grandmothers showing up without a viable reason for copious amounts of alcohol to be present – like Cinco de Mayo – then those good-natured maple syrup-loving folk had better run. Abuelas were the one thing everyone could be in agreement to fear.

Cora plopped down on her couch and stretched out. Home at last! Not for long, though. It was only a matter of time before her sanctuary was tainted, especially if she tried to ditch dinner. This was the one thing she knew her mother would never forgive her for, and there was the real threat of her mother driving over here to drag her to dinner. Cora was too depressed after the long day at work to find the will power to go on living, much less face her family. Maybe her hot boyfriend would know what she should do, or at least could offer some encouragement about going to dinner. Again, she fell into that place where she was probably labeling Dylan premature, but it just came too naturally.

Note to self: Define relationship with Dylan.

Now probably wasn't the right time to do that. She didn't have much will power or optimism to handle the thought that defining Dylan might not result in him being her boyfriend. Dylan might just be her sexy boy toy. No, that just sounded weird. And what even was a boy toy? It sounded like he was something to play with, but Cora couldn't imagine how other than sexually. Naw, it was probably best to down play it and keep it realistic versus play it up as a relationship only to be crushed. It was a lot easier to just refer to Dylan as her boyfriend and end that mental debate. Besides, who wanted to walk around admitting they were single and just hanging out with a hot guy?

Got a family thin. Save me?

Whats a family thin? Killin em off so shrinkin fam?

Cora laughed at his text. He'd been better at replying faster. It definitely felt like there was something more to their relationship now. Maybe Dylan really had the boyfriend status, and maybe she should upgrade that to sexy boyfriend status.

No but I might. Family dinner. Grandma here. Don't want to go.

It wasn't like she was begging him to ask her out before their actual second date. Just being an alibi would be enough to help, not that her family was actually going to go through the effort of calling Dylan to check. But Cora couldn't help but see this as a way to answer the epic debate.

Gonna b asking why Im not married… if I got a man…

She waited to see if he'd take the bait and label himself. It was way too soon to be talking about the serious side if that text, but it should be enough to feel him out. Maybe she could see where his mind was at and see if he could joke and flirt with the idea of being her boyfriend. Or maybe he would just laugh, and Cora would get the feeling that he really didn't see her as anything but a warm body. But if he wrote back that it was okay to call him her boyfriend, nothing would really change other than it would suddenly be perfect. Perfect for her mentally and perfect because that's what she wanted them to end up being – boyfriend and girlfriend. If Dylan flaked, then it looked like she would be free to cancel their Thai dinner date without guilt. It was free food, but why would she waste her time when it clearly had been a joke the whole time?

She give you hell, call me n I'll deal wit her :)

Cora tried not to squeal. It wasn't the answer that she was hoping for, but it definitely was on the side of something. If she did need to call him, then he'd have to answer the questions that her family was peppering her with – and he knew those type of questions. Dylan could be painfully honest and say they're "just friends" but that wasn't going to save her. He would have to admit to being Cora's boyfriend. That would be the only way to save her and he had to know that before he volunteered. Then again, he probably knew that it would never come to that.

Cranky old woman yellin at ya? Hope ur Spanish is good.

Probably should hope that her crazy abuela didn't end up scaring him off. Dylan might be able to talk the talk, but her abuela could scare the life into the dead. She'd seen it firsthand when they thought her uncle had passed away. Abuela Mariza went over to the wake at their house, yelled at him some threats about joining him in the afterlife to haunt his soul unless he got his ass back here, and then poured her glass of sparkling cider over his corpse. Uncle Julio was never the same after that. The doctors still didn't know how he came back after being dead for two days, but they never met her abuela.

Sounds like my kinda woman – feisty

Oh. My. God.

Cora really hoped that he meant that in a way of coming around to her and not that her abuela turned him on. Like, he was going to be into Cora because feistiness was in her DNA. It was either that or admit that Dylan had a thing for grandmas, and that was taking one step closer to the creepier side. She tried not to gag over that thought while she quickly disposed the cellphone in her purse. There was no way she was touching that text with a ten-and-a-half-foot digital pole.

She had too much to go before suffering through this family dinner, and she couldn't afford giving Dylan's text another minute. She had to shower and change into more appropriate clothing for the Fiesta de la Abuela Mariza. That would take all night just to undo all the work that Cora had put into her appearance this morning. She would have the dry her hair and make sure it stayed curly. She would have to throw on a red lip and draw up some dramatic eye make-up. Basically, Cora needed to dig up something with enough flare and sex appeal to prove that she was a Latina, but still have the modesty factor of someone who was unmarried. This was why she wasn't going to survive another Valencia family event. Impossible was impossible.

All her sisters were sporting flowy gauze skirts in the brightest patterns Cora had ever seen. She hoped that this wasn't a permanent side effect of Tropical Storm Mariza and wouldn't see her as a victim too. The damage had even spread to the males of the family, brother-in-laws included. They weren't forced into the lively skirts, but they were dressed rather stereotypically in khaki pants and Latin flavored shirts. Meanwhile, abuela sat in her chair with more subdued hues and patterns. She looked almost out of place in the mayhem caused solely by her and for her.

Cora had managed to find a long, flowy skirt to pair with a white peasant blouse. It was nowhere near as obnoxious as her sister's outfits, but it wasn't something that was Cora. That was one of the blessings of wearing "white folk" clothes – aka things that looked normal – and being the youngest which meant having slightly more leeway with the elders. Of course, it only gained jealous glares from her sisters. She might not be the most successful of her family, but Cora was definitely one of the bright ones.

"Hola, Abuela Mariza." She waved and made a beeline for the old woman. It was best to get the obligatory hug out of the way and then go hide in obscurity, in peace. That was the game plan until the old woman got a hold of her. For someone a zillion years old, she had the strength of a twenty-something body builder.

"Where is my grandbaby's handsome man?" Abuela asked in Spanish.

Cora couldn't mistranslate that. There was no "handsome man" that she would have brought, minus Dylan, but that would be submitting him to torture too. Clearly her abuela was very blind and wasn't realizing who she was talking to or she was just really confused. "Abuela, I'm not Xo. Tommy's outside with his son and papa."

She clearly confused Cora for her more flamboyant older sister, Xiomara. How that was even possible was beyond her. Unlike Cora, Xo loved and lived her culture to the extreme. She had been able to see her sister a mile away, at the bus stop. Xo definitely had the brightest outfit of the day and had the loud Spanish voice that carried.

"Little Coriara, I'm looking for your man," the shrill voice scolded. "It is time to marry and have a family."

It was a new record for abuela. She had lasted almost a full minute before hounding her about marrying someone and becoming a blissful domestic slave to his children. A future that she had tried, repetitively, to convince her abuela of otherwise. Every time, Cora was scolded for not wanting all that not and lectured for hours about how important a husband and children were to the family. Unfortunately, the visits were few enough and far between that the old woman forgot their argument. Abuela kept bringing it up every time, but maybe it was less forgetfulness and more pushing Cora towards what the family wanted. The definition of insanity was repeating something and hoping for different results. Maybe it was time to step away from the insanity.

"Dylan couldn't make it, abuela. He had a big meeting at work."

There was zero reaction on abuela's face, to Cora's disappointment. There were, however, a couple gasps from the surrounding family members. It clearly wasn't what they had expected to hear, and it was news to all of them. But was it really that crazy that she might have a boyfriend? After all their badgering throughout the years, was it so unrealistic to think that it might actually happen someday? God, it was like her whole family thought she was some ugly loser that would be single for her whole life.

Her abuela started to speak again, but it was time to put into plan Operation Escape Plan Delta Sigma Go. Cora reached for her phone, thinking up an excuse on the fly. "Oh, my phone was on vibrate. I didn't realize it. Dylan tried calling and I missed him. I really got to call him back right now."

She hurried down the hall away from the commotion, and into her old bedroom. Well, her sisters and her old room, seeing as they all shared it. No one else was there, which was such a relief. On one bed, there was a pile of jackets, diaper bags, and purses. Some shoes littered the floor from relatives that chose not to have the wrath of her mother rain down on them for tracking in dirt from outside. It wasn't the best hideaway, but at least it was quiet.

5min before you came up

She texted Dylan. At least she had that distraction. He could help her escape until dinner was on the table and everyone was too busy stuffing their faces to talk. She'd have to figure out a way to smuggle a couple hot homemade rolls in her purse for later.

Must be a record. U lasted 2 long :P

That got Cora laughing. He had no idea how big of a record that was with her family. She stared at the screen and his words, feeling a bit melancholy. Rereading his text, it felt like he was holding something back. It didn't seem like a normal Dylan text, not that she had the vast knowledge to categorize the varying degrees and meanings of everything pertaining to Dylan. She actually missed his sexually charged flirting, which was more surprising to Cora.

You last long, right? Don't leave a girl disappointed ;)

It was probably the worst thing she could have wrote at the moment, but it seemed like a good idea – and a fast way – to get the old Dylan back. It was nice to have him to talk to, but it was more of a distraction if he was flirty. It would fry her mind and completely distract her. Besides, they'd have to bring up the sex talk eventually. Now seemed almost like as good of time as any. She was stuck here with nowhere better to run to for a while.

Babe U kno it :D

That was something she really wasn't sure she needed to know. Well, she did but she didn't. So, when and if they got to that point, it wasn't going to be over after a thrust or two. Either Dylan would have no idea what to do or he would know exactly what to do – which then meant that she wanted him to last that long. Talking to Dylan and knowing how he acted, she was sure it was the latter. Clarice's opinion seemed to back that, even if it was just based on her delusions – Dylan was a stud.

The only bad thing about his text was that it was a dud in the conversation department. It was just a statement, and a statement didn't really further the conversation along. She could question it, but Cora could only imagine the can of worms it would open up. Did she really want to do this while they both knew she was at her parent's house, which could raise up a multitude of awkward situations? Well, she already shot that to shit when she started texting him. Cora was already alone and probably in a place where she was going to be ignored for an hour or so. It probably would have been better if she had started this talk at home. But hindsight was twenty-twenty.

So, with Dylan in limbo between the sexual innuendos and being obviously available, Cora did the only thing that made sense. She started the sex talk. However, it was probably the worst possible way to ease into it, and against her better judgement.

How?

Okay, so it was slightly awkward. More like probing to see how he saw her rather than to really dive into his secrets. Maybe Dylan was into dosing. From what she heard, that little blue pill was basically a miracle you swallowed.

Rvrse CGirl. Let U set th pace
Flip U over n get ur legs over my shoulders
Grind in2 da swet pussy
Hard n long. All nite
Git u cuming hard

Oh, dear god almighty and the seven great holy avocadoes.

Dylan had mistaken what she meant and gone full-on porno on her screen. Maybe it was her mistake in not wording that better. She had only been curious about how someone could last long. Like did they stop halfway and go make a sandwich, then come back to finish? She hadn't been clear about the "how", but Cora surely hadn't meant for this turn of events – especially when it seemed like she was the star in his fantasy. That alone made her blush, but then she couldn't help picturing it and get turned on by what he'd do.

Cora had no idea what to do now that there was a lull in the texts. Should she send an emoji? Was this her turn to go into explicit detail over their imaginary exploits? God, she hoped not. There was no way that she could make anything sound convincing, and she wasn't sure that she wanted to write anything like that back to him. What could she even say? Put the D inside me? That wasn't the same level as his texts and maybe he'd see her as a fraud. Her phone beeped again with another message and it seemed like she wouldn't have to worry about texting back.

Quiet cos ur cummin?

Cora swallowed hard. She knew that this was a slippery slope. If she admitted the truth, then that would probably say far more about herself than she was comfortable sharing with him right now. Cora could always use the excuse of her family interrupting as the reason she didn't respond for like, three hours, and take the heat off. But then she'd still probably have to confess or lie later about how it made her feel. He would probably be fishing to know if that was something she was into or not because he was hoping to deliver on it. There didn't seem like an easy way out. There was only one real way out – to use what Dylan gave her.

Yea

He sent a smiley face emoji a second later. Cora though that was the end of it until he started texting her again.

Me 2. Can't wait 4 U

Shit.

Chapter Four

Dylan said to keep it simple. It was going to be dinner at his place, but what did simple mean? Jeans and a t-shirt came to mind, but a dress seemed more date appropriate. A dress might be too presumptuous though, given the texts that had transpired, and the type of guy Dylan was when he joked around. She'd have to wear leggings too, but that created a whole new dilemma in the shoe department. Flats would take away the height boost and make the difference between her and Dylan greater. It would leave the awkward mid-section hug for affectionate gestures. Boots would be the best – and the one Cora would probably end up going with – but then that limited her dress choices because of their lengths. These were serious fashion decisions that she'd to make, and Dylan obviously had no idea if he thought all this was simple.

Brown shimmer club eyeliner, her Urban Decay eye palette, false eyelashes, mascara, and a red lip. That was her go-to date look. The false lashes could be nixed easily. Maybe a nude lip would be better instead of a full-on red lip. That shimmery brown eyeliner though was subtle enough – in her mind – and brought out the honey tones in her brown eyes. And who went with bare eyelids? Simple. Cora had somehow managed to keep it simple. Okay – eyeliner, light neutral eye shadow, and a nude lip. That should look simple to Dylan, but what he didn't know wouldn't be held against her.

Her hair was the easiest part. For once, her Hispanic roots had a perk – it gave her hair a sexy, natural curl. And curls went with almost every look in the book. Unlike their first date, they wouldn't be outside where she could blame imperfections on a stray wind or from bending over to grab a golf ball.

Her cellphone started ringing. Cora practically jumped over her futon to get to it in time before the call went to voicemail. She hadn't thought that it might be Dylan calling to cancel. Well, she didn't think about that until she got her phone off the charger in the kitchen. It was much worse than that. Cora saw the caller ID on the screen. Her family did not fit into her plans for the day. There wasn't enough time, and Cora was sure if there was another long story or lecture that was going to come from this call. No doubt it would alter her mood and that would carry over into her date. Dylan would probably ask if there was something wrong and that would start the downward spiral of either lies or being the girl with the crazy family you knew that you needed to escape from before getting lost in that special brand of insanity.

She let her mother's call go to voicemail. That wasn't the end of it, Cora knew it. A minute later, her older sister called. Then her younger sister. Her brother-in-law. Her cousin. Her mother again. If Cora didn't know her family

– or any Hispanic clan – she would have been worried that something serious had happened in her family. No, it wasn't something important and it definitely wasn't going to stop. It was probably a bickering fight going on at home over something petty and they were desperately calling to get her on their side before the others called and pulled her onto their team. It was probably over something equally irrelevant as which brand of tortillas should be used at the next family event seeing as abuela called out her sister on burning – ever so slightly – the handmade tortillas yesterday. Wounded pride and catty fights were not simple and did not match her outfit today.

Cora put her cellphone on vibrate, after debating shutting it off. The problem was if Dylan tried to contract her, he wouldn't be able to get through. At least with it set on vibrate, she could see all his messages or calls on the lock screen. She needed to get ready and then check out the bus schedules to figure out which route she needed to take to get to Dylan's apartment. Probably not the smartest thing to leave it until the day of, but Cora hadn't been too confident that this date was actually going to happen. That wasn't something that she needed to think of right now. Cora set down the phone and went to finish getting ready for her big dinner date.

It was exciting though – the whole dating process. It was a hassle to sit through hours of preening and polishing just for an hour or two with some guy. The excitement was in knowing that there was a date and that there was a guy out there that was just as excited as you were about it. Dylan wanted to see her, and she got the chance to be a five-year-old girl again and play dress-up until she found the perfect outfit Cora had a night to dress up, feel good, and, in the very least, get an awesome new profile photo from the selfie she was sure to take later. A girl had to capitalize on her "fancy" time. Plus, her younger sister just uploaded one of herself in a bikini and there was no sane reason Cora would either A) squeeze into one of those torture devices, and B) be upstaged by her younger sister of all people. She couldn't not put up a better profile photo now.

The weather was rather nice when Cora headed out of the house. The sun was out at least and there wasn't a terrible wind. It definitely was good to see that the weather wasn't going to completely mess up her hair. No, she'd leave that to Dylan and his body. She had stashed one of the new DVD releases from the library into her purse. Dinner and then snuggle time on the couch. Either his arm or the back of the couch was going to mess up her perfect hair and cause a frizzle or two to escape the hair spray.

She headed down the street to where the bus was. The bus shouldn't be much longer. According to the schedule, if it was on time, it would be along in only a minute or two. Three minutes at most. There weren't many people waiting at this bus stop either, which was nice. There would be no forced small talk and no weirdos trying to talk to her, so there was going to be no need to plan how to escape and avoid them on the bus ride. Just in case – could one jump out of a moving bus or did the doors lock once the bus moved? The questionable looking public transit bus rolled up to the stop. With no one getting off, Cora was quick to hop on with the hope of finding a seat alone and not having to balance her attention between escaping and texting Dylan. She deposited her fare token and was pleasantly surprised to find there were seats open, even if they were all the way in the back. She barely made it halfway through the bus when it kicked into motion and merged back into the sometimes scary traffic found in downtown Boston. Gripping the overhead hand rails, she safely wobbled into a seat without falling into anyone or knocking over anyone's cup of Dunkin' Donut coffee.

On my way over. Be there in 30

At least she would be if the traffic stayed light and the bus was able to stick to the schedule. Maybe she should have added a ten-minute buffer just to be on the safe side. Cora would want someone to give her an accurate time, or even be early, if she was meeting up with someone. Otherwise, she would be worried that something happened to them – like were they kidnapped or maimed or injured – or did they decide to ditch her?

Cora tried not to think of that. She didn't want to get into a negative mindset when she was about to meet up with Dylan for their date. Although, after a while, there was still no reply from Dylan. He knew today was their date. It was only yesterday that he was reminded of that, and it wasn't that long after their first date. He couldn't claim to have forgot her, but he could have found someone better to focus his energy on pursuing. Although there had to be some unwritten dating rule that said he needed to at least attempt to remember dates. She could understand if it was months or years after they started dating and it was one of their many anniversaries that he forgot. There were years between those events, not days. Try as she might, she couldn't stop thinking the worst. At least she managed to stop herself from sending another text after another text until he eventually cracked and typed something back.

When she was one bus stop away and hadn't heard anything from him, Cora started to plan her way out of this. She had a feeling that she was getting ditched. There was always the option to just ride the bus to the end of the line and stay on it as it weaved its way back along the route. Chances were that she could get out of the additional fare if she just explained her misfortunes or tried to hide under the seats. It really wouldn't cost her anything more than she had planned, seeing as she was going to pay a return fare after the dinner date – if it happened at all. The biggest problem would be telling Dylan that she couldn't make it or that something came up. She wasn't the best at lying and it probably wouldn't end up sounding legit. Although, if he was ditching her, then it wouldn't matter. At that point Cora knew that she could never reach out or talk to him ever again, but she wasn't sure simply deleting his phone number would be enough. The challenge would be sticking to that plan. He wasn't really worth the time of day that Cora was giving him. It was just that after the first date, she expected more from him and this relationship, and she let it all get under her skin. A relationship that she was going to downgrade the instant the bus pulled away and approached Dylan's bus stop. There was no way that this was a relationship; it was a... sweet and great one!

Dylan was waiting at the bus stop with a bundle of flowers in his hands. He hadn't forgotten! In fact, he was a real Prince Charming. A huge, silly smile grew on Cora's face as she got up and all but ran off the bus to leap into his arms. She didn't leap in his arms, but she did get off and lean up to kiss his cheek.

"Oh, hey." He smiled down at her. There was a bit of mischief in his eyes. "You better not let my girl see you doing that. I'm supposed to meet her and woo her with these flowers."

Cora rolled her eyes. He was always the jokester. "Guess I should have been more sneaky then. I wouldn't want you to get in trouble."

He laughed and pulled her in for a kiss. Wow... There was just a quick peck after their first date, but that had nothing on this. This one actually felt like something. This was a real kiss. It puzzled her like no other because it wasn't something that she had expected. Dylan laughed again at the obviously shocked expression.

"Yea, babe. I'm that good." He winked.

It took Cora a while for her to get a thought back. The first one was wondering how, and when, the flowers came to be in her hands. She didn't remember taking them from Dylan. The second thought was that Dylan really sounded cocky with that comment, but that was immediately followed by a warm and fuzzy feeling. His hand had slipped into hers as they walked down the sideward towards his place.

"So, how was the bus ride?" It was small talk, but she let herself believe that Dylan really did care.

Cora shrugged. "I've had worse. There were actually open seats, which was more surprising."

She tried to take note of the places they were passing. It seemed like a nice little neighborhood. This was a part of town that Cora had ruled out when she was looking into places to rent during her great escape from home. This neighborhood was out because it was slightly difficult to get to for her family. Cora knew how much input her family had on her life, and her choice of apartments was no different. The main reason, though, for nixing this neighborhood was the cost.

"Did you know that it's possible to get on a bus and make it through a whole ride without seeing someone with blue hair or a crazy outfit?" Dylan laughed at her joke, just like she had hoped. It felt much better to get him laughing on purpose rather than at something she was making a semi-serious comment about – or just anything she did.

He shook his head. "I wouldn't believe you. Although, it's usually not blue hair that would surprise me. It's more of purple hair and rainbow mohawks. That usually is only at risk of happening when that fantasy convention is going on downtown at the convention center and the weirdos come out."

There was just something about the tone in Dylan's voice when he said that which made her uneasy. That was just some event for people who like those types of things and it was their hobby. There really was nothing wrong with it. It was practically the same as following the Bruins or the Patriots and collecting sport memorabilia and being able to recite team factoids from the past thirty years. To her, it was the same thing.

Dylan just seemed to be a judging person. If he was that judgmental and selective of whom he was around, that meant she passed the test and met his obviously high standards. As much as Cora never wanted to admit that she liked having validation from someone else, especially one of the male population, it felt great and she loved it. Even if Dylan's general view on other people was a shitty, judgmental one.

"So, where's your place?" It seemed like they had been walking for quite a few blocks now. She had decent shoes on, but this was really more exercise than she had hoped. She didn't want to end up sweating and smelly.

"Just there. Third floor." Dylan gestured up ahead. He glanced her way with almost a sad expression on his face. "Elevator's out right now, so it's a three-floor walk-up."

That got a groan out of her. If the elevator was out, why didn't he warn her sooner or try to reschedule? Cora wasn't exactly in shape. Exercise was so low on her list of things to do and there were so many more important television shows to catch up on, like *The Royals* and everything on BBC America. The new season of *Sherlock* was going to be starting and there was no way that she could miss a second of that amazing show, or that sexy British man playing the lead – Ben Cumberland or something like that. There was probably a zero percent chance, though, that she could get Dylan to carry her up all those stairs.

The building was a rather nice brownstone. There were little garden beds by the doors and a few of the windows going up were spotted with small planters of flowers and greenery. It didn't really seem like the place Dylan would live. She imagined more of a fraternity house, not some respectable family dwelling. Maybe his apartment would better reflect that. For all she knew, he had some kind of an in with the landlord or inherited this beauty of a building. Inside, it was just as nice. It was obvious that this had been a relic of Boston but was remodeled and done up right on the inside to still hold that same bit of character, in just nicer amenities. Of course, pass the rows of mailboxes was the elevator with a yellow sign warning that it was out of service and dooming the patrons to flights of stairs.

"Have you lived here long?" Okay, it was time to be a little nosey. Dylan had checked his mailbox and now they had the challenging stairwell to conquer.

"Nah, just a couple of years. I just wanted something close to work and this just happened to open up at the time."

So that ruled out obscure rich relatives or generations of rent-controlled leases. The way it sounded was like the amount of rent a place like this cost was nothing. Cora could hardly think the same way. Even if they moved in down the road when they were in their "long-term relationship" phase, this still wouldn't be an inconvenience to her. It was further from her family and an excuse not to go to work because of her "sugar daddy". There were so many pros to Dylan and, honestly, not a lot of cons. He just needed to lose the judging tone sometimes, but she could help him fix that. That would be easy enough to do if she just brought it to his attention.

"Sounds like you got lucky."

Dylan threw a smile her way. "In more ways than one."

Ugh, he was such a flirt! Maybe that was something Cora needed to fix too. It was something that roped her into a first date with the guy. It was kind of cute back then, but it seemed like it would get old.

He stopped at apartment three fourteen and stuck the key into the door. She noted the Patriot charm on his keyring. Dylan was probably one of those crazy fans – just like her brother-in-law. Maybe later Cora could actually put to use the pointless trivia he sprouted off at the last family gathering. At least it might earn her some brownie points with Dylan. Maybe those family gatherings weren't a complete and total waste of time.

Cora walked into his apartment and was impressed. It was rather clean, for a single guy. The loft-style had a nice open area concept that gave her a wide view of the whole place, minus the bedroom which she guessed was behind one of the three doors. The one closest to her turned out to be just a closet. That meant one of the remaining two was the bathroom, so it was easy to figure which was which. That definitely would reduce the chance of her looking like an idiot and she wouldn't need to ask for a tour, which may be more awkward. Cora knew that she wanted to stay away from any room that had a bed in it. The last thing she wanted to give Dylan was the wrong idea and asking for a tour might seem like she was begging for the bedroom. Flirting was fine. Mattress mamboing wasn't.

"It's going to take a bit for the Pad Thai to finish cooking. I have some curry that I could heat up now if you're hungry. Could always skip right to dessert." Dylan winked at her. He was being flirty again, but there was that sexual hint under it all. She doubted any realistic dessert would be more than an instant pudding mix or some store-bought cookies.

Cora rolled her eyes when he wasn't looking. "I can wait."

Curry didn't sound as appetizing right now. Worst case scenario, she didn't want to get sick on Thai food before actually trying his Thai food. Really, curry was like the fake version of Thai food. And wasn't that an Indian thing? Pad Thai was the real stuff; after all, it had "Thai" right in its name.

"Do you need any help?" She had no idea how long this could take to make. Why not help? It would be like a little glimpse into their future together, and it would kill some time. Unlike her Latina sisters, Cora wanted and expected her husband to be helping out in the kitchen with the cooking. She wasn't born to be a slave to any man. She believed in equality. Just like she accepted the disgusting fact that she'd probably have to take out the trash once or twice in her life. Besides, cooking really wasn't her forte and she'd rather not starve the rest of her life.

Dylan stuck his hands in the pockets of his jeans and seemed to consider it for a moment. "Why don't you just chill on the couch? Find a movie or something on Netflix."

Well, if he didn't want her help then there was no point in forcing the issue. Maybe this was just another perk of being with Dylan. He'd end up pampering her and actually treating her like she was something precious and not just some girl he could quickly walk away from.

She grabbed the remote off the coffee table as she sat down on the couch, which was really nice and plush. She set the flowers down where the remote had been – realizing that they were still in her possession – and turned on the television. "Is there anything in particular that you like to watch?"

Cora could handle biting the bullet to watch something that she wasn't interested in, but this was his apartment and she didn't want to bore him to death. It was the least that she could do when he was cooking and giving her a break to just relax. And this was a comfortable place and this perfect couch to do that.

"You."

She looked at him over the back of the couch. Clearly Cora had heard him wrong. He had to be joking, but he looked dead serious. It made the butterflies in her stomach flutter and sent a chill up her spine with that little glint in his eye. Admitting that he liked to watch her wasn't something that she couldn't take as flirty. It felt like Dylan wanted to see more of her than he could right now and to watch what she would do. That look made her feel like prey and that he wanted to watch her beneath him.

After a moment, he broke the building tension. "But anything sports or some action thing would be good."

Cora nodded. She couldn't shake the feeling that one word caused. Flipping through the channels, there wasn't anything that really interested her in the slightest and nothing that wouldn't bore the both of them to death. She was thinking that it was time to give up and just pick a channel with her eyes closed when a loud bang came from the kitchen. It made her jump and she glanced over at Dylan, staring at the floor and just shaking his head.

"You okay over there?"

"Of course I am, babe." He sighed and rolled his eyes.

Dylan just seemed to brush off her concern as he bent down to pick up the two pans that had slipped and clamored on the floor. Cora saw that he kept them stacked on top of the fridge. He must have been going for one when the stack shifted and grew unstable, then came tumbling down. At least it didn't seem like he was hurt anywhere, except maybe his ego.

The odd thing was that Cora found herself checking out his ass again as he bent to retrieve the pans. Usually she wouldn't have cared or thought about looking. She was more of a bright eyes and sparkling smile type of gal. And, of course, it was her first real trip south of the border and she got caught.

"Like what you see, babe?" Dylan laughed, clearly amused. Cora felt her face heat up from embarrassment. She was willing to bet that she was redder than a tomato. Meanwhile, his wounded pride seemed to have recovered. He was probably telling himself that this was what he had planned to do the whole time. "I'd be happy to show you more."

Oh, god, no! ... but oh please, yes!

She whipped her head back around and stared at the television while she tried to catch her cool. There was no way that she could handle all that right now. This had to be another one of his little games to get her to tumble head over heels for him.

She couldn't help but steal glances over at the kitchen. Dylan had his back to her, most of the time. It seemed like he actually knew how to cook judging by the aromas he could create. They were mouthwatering. While the remote had chosen something with action and booms, Cora's eyes were more focused on peeking over the back of the couch like some little kid that wasn't tall enough to see all the way over or like some spy or creeper.

"What's that?" She asked meekly.

Dylan turned around and laughed when he saw her. She didn't care this time – that was how good it smelled. "I told you, babe, it's Pad Thai. I just tossed in the red peppers and the sauce. That's what you're smelling."

He cracked another panty dropping smile before dipping the wooden spoon into the pan. Dylan caught a tiny bite and walked over to the couch, offering it to her. She leaned in to take a taste. "You like that, babe?"

Cora nodded. Maybe he was talking about the food he was cooking. Maybe he was talking about the image of him cooking. Maybe he was talking about the sexual hints he was dropping. Regardless of what Dylan was really trying to say, the food was good.

"Is it almost ready?"

It hadn't been that long since she got here but Chinese food always was delivered super quick. So that meant that it didn't take long to make, in her mind. They definitely slung out orders fast at the food trucks downtown. And Thailand was close enough to China to be lumped together in their culinary time constraints.

"You really like it then." Dylan smiled and turned his back to her for a moment to push things around the pan again. "It's close. Probably just a couple more minutes and it'll be good. I got a couple Sam Adams in the fridge, if you want to grab them."

She wondered why beers were brought up. Maybe that was all he had to drink, or he just wanted to make sure they were relaxed. Cora could see the kitchen sink and doubted that it was just there for show. He probably didn't have anything else to offer, and she couldn't really hold that against him. Dylan didn't seem like the kind of guy to keep Kool-Aid or some "from frozen concentrate" fruit juice. She could be giving him too much of the benefit of doubt, and maybe he was hoping to get her tipsy and sneak into her panties.

"Water is fine for me. Don't want to drink all your beers." Cora got up and walked into the kitchen. "Where do you keep your glasses?"

Dylan pointed to one of the cupboards. She opened it to find a stack of red plastic cups and a handful of sport glasses. She skipped the frat boy staple – it felt like sacrilege seeing as she wasn't going to be filling it with alcohol – and went for a Patriots glass. She moved around Dylan and filled up the glass in the sink. When she tried to step away, Cora found herself stuck. He had wrapped his arm around her waist to keep her beside him as he finished up the dish.

She glanced up at him with a questioning look. What was he doing? He just smiled down at her like he was innocent in all this and like that hand on her hip didn't belong to him. Cora opened her mouth to ask why he ensnared her, but she found his lips on hers – and his tongue slipping into her mouth.

Cora tried not to panic. She had kissed a guy before, but those were more planned and obviously coming at the time. She never had such a surprise attack before, and she had never kissed anyone with tongue before. It felt strange, and invading, and why was it just wiggling around?! Her tongue had struck back against the invader on its own accord, but his was stroking the roof of her mouth in a "come hither" fashion. Maybe if she tried to poke it, it would go away. Cora missed and ended up sliding her tongue along the underside of his tongue. Dylan groaned and something clattered on the floor as his other arm wrapped around Cora to pull her body against his body. She could feel something growing between them, and it wasn't her feelings for him. Her mind told her to shove Dylan back, but he had already broke it off and took a step back.

"Damn." His eyes stared on her mouth as he licked his lips. There was a smirk on his face, and it seemed like this might have all been part of the plan – which seemed to have gone according to plan. If only he knew what Cora was thinking, but that didn't matter. He leaned in to place a quick peck on her lips before she could think of some verbal slaps to give him after that.

"We'll have to save that for later, babe." With that, he let her go.

Cora wobbled a little with her first steps of freedom. Maybe she was blowing this all out of context. The uneasy steps were less to do with his kissing skills and more with just being completely blindsided by the encounter. Coming to his place and all was definitely a poor idea, and it was obvious that Dylan had completely different things on his mind than she did tonight. She just wanted to have dinner and try this Thai food thing.

She made her way back to the couch and sat down, staring off at the television but not really seeing it. Her mind was a bit fuzzy. She was knocked off balance and she was pretty sure that she didn't like it. Cora reached for the glass of water, hoping that taking a sip of it might help her get things back together.

The stove clicked in the other room and there was cupboard door thudding shut. There were sounds of plates tinging against each other and then footsteps. Dylan placed two plates of food on the coffee table in front of them and sat down.

"I have some bad news." He sighed. "It seems that we knocked over the pan that had the pine nuts roasting when we got hot in the kitchen. I mean, it's basically still Pad Thai. It won't be the full experience."

"Oh, okay," Cora said quietly, giving him a slight nod like she was understanding. There was steam still raising up from the food in front of them. It was a whirl of noodles with peppers with shrimp. To her, everything looked fine. Cora wasn't sure that she really was missing out on anything without the nuts. "I'm sure it'll still taste good."

"So, no regrets, then?" He asked, reaching for his plate.

It wasn't very clear what he meant. Did she regret not having the pine nuts? It's hard to regret losing something that you never had. So, she shook her head. "No regrets."

That made him smile.

Cora followed his lead and brought the plate to rest on her lap. She used the fork to twirl some noodles around it before stabbing some of the peppers to keep it all from unraveling. It wasn't something that really was new. Other than maybe tasting a hint of peanut butter, this was basically Chinese food. The shrimp was a nice touch, but she didn't know if that was supposed to really be there or if he tried to make the noodles fancy. She tried one of those and it was really good.

"You really know how to cook. I'm impressed." Like, really impressed. Cora had never dated a guy that could do much more than operate a microwave and call in take-out orders.

"Thanks, but this isn't that hard." She wondered if that was a hint of blushing or if it was a trick of the television lighting his face. Maybe Dylan wasn't always the cocky and sure type of guy that he came off as being. "I bet you can cook a lot better food than this. It's practically in your blood."

It was what?

There were two ways that she could take that. One, that she was Hispanic and that's all her "people" could do – other than clean rich people's homes and farm. The second one was that he assumed because she was a woman that she was the better cook. Not escaping the stereotypes, but at least it wasn't racist. Dylan didn't seem to catch on to what he said, nor did he notice that she was having internal dialogue. It must have been innocent, and she was just taking it the wrong way and to the extreme. Bringing it up could risk ruining this date. The best thing would be to give him the benefit of the doubt and let it go.

"I'm actually not that much of a cook. I don't really have time to cook." That was a stretch. More like she purposely didn't leave any time to cook before she got hungry, then ran down to the store or grab a burger somewhere.

"So, you're not going to cook for me?" He glanced over at her.

Cora shook her. "Not unless you want to die. I'm pretty bad. I wouldn't advise it."

That and she didn't really want to have to cook. That was too much work. If Dylan was cooking, she'd have no problem helping and she could almost promise that she wouldn't chop off a finger – which Cora told him as much. He did laugh, but it was odd.

"So, you like basketball?" He asked, nodding towards the television.

Again, Cora shook her head. "No, but it was the only actiony thing that was on. Wait, do you hate it?"

"No." He took another bite of the Pad Thai. "I'm not a big fan but I like to watch a game every now and then. Just wondered if you did too. You know, that whole "getting to know you" thing. Someone told me that I should try it because I may have been being difficult before."

She laughed because she knew that Dylan meant her. "Oh, really? Well, I think it's a good idea."

He shook his head and reached for the beer. It was enough of an action to get her to notice, and it made her mind wander. Had Dylan been nice before when he offered her one or was, he hoping for something else? He did seem different tonight, but almost in a good way until that one thing... Cora knew that she overthought a lot in relationships. Maybe it was all just in her head and she was still trying to psych herself out. Maybe she should have just taken the offered beer so that she could have relaxed.

"So, how'd you learn to make Thai?" Cora asked, hoping to maybe learn something.

He shrugged. "Just from a YouTube video. I got tired of going downtown to get good takeout."

The home team scored just moments before the buzzer. Dylan cheered and nearly spilled his plate of food when he jumped up. Not a big fan? Yea, Cora didn't think so anymore. He definitely was a big fan.

Cora took the last bite of the Pad Thai and held her hand out for his plate. "Seeing as you cooked, the least I can do is the dishes as a sign of gratitude."

"Not what I had in mind." He handed over the plate. "I do have a dishwasher, so you're getting off easy."

"Oh." She hadn't known that. Now it didn't really seem like that big of deal to wash them.

Dylan had followed her into the kitchen. "Well, this was a date so I'm not expecting you to do anything but enjoy yourself. I want you to like it here and be comfortable. Especially with me."

That was a little strange to say, but she thought that she knew what Dylan meant. He just meant that he hoped she was comfortable around him because they'd be seeing a lot of each other while they dated. Maybe it just was his way of saying that he wanted to see more of her.

"I am comfortable with you, Dylan." Hopefully that would set his mind at ease. Maybe he'd been acting a bit off because he had been so worried about that. "And I do like it here. You got a great place."

He leaned in for a rather chaste kiss. "Can you stay longer, or do you need to catch a bus?"

Cora knew that there was a late bus, but she had never taken it. There were horror stories about the late-late bus, and it really felt like he was giving her an option to run away now. While she had a nice dinner date, Cora wasn't so sure what they'd do if she stuck around longer. He definitely wouldn't like the stuff that she binge watched on Netflix and it wasn't acceptable just to lay on that couch surfing the internet on her phone. Plus, her comfy pajamas were at home and it would be a judge-free zone about what she looked like. There was no one at home to impress – not even a goldfish or houseplant.

"I don't really want to eat and dash, but I should probably catch this next bus. Is that alright?"

Dylan nodded. "Yea, let me walk you out."

She followed him out of the apartment and down the three flights of stairs. It definitely was nicer going down than it was walking up that. Hopefully the elevator would be fixed by the next time she came around. The air was a little cooler when they stepped out, and Cora hadn't thought to wear something a little warmer. Although, her jean jacket was doing an okay job, but it still let a chill go down her neck. Maybe Dylan noticed, or maybe he didn't, but he wrapped an arm around her shoulders, and they strolled to the bus stop.

"So, have are you a fan of Thai food now?" He asked as they stepped under the bus stop spotlight.

"I don't know." Cora knew that she probably could make that sound more flirty than it did, but she was a little tired after all that. Plus, having a big meal like that in her tummy was making her crave a nap. "I'd probably eat it again. Does that count?"

Dylan nodded. "And what do you think of me?"

Oh... that was a heavy-hitting question. Cora knew that she liked him but hadn't really thought much passed that. Of course, she could instantly think of their imaginary future together, but that version of Dylan was all in her head. She was really only just starting to get to know who he was. So far, he wasn't that bad. He was a little more forward than she had expected and compared to what she was used to with her exes. But that might not be a bad thing.

"I think I like you."

"I think I like you too."

The headlights flashed them as it turned the corner and rolled to a stop. Cora was a little disappointed that it was actually running on time. It meant that she had to get on and leave Dylan, even if it was just for a moment. They could always text.

"Well, that's my bus so... I guess I should get on it." Her voice didn't sound too thrilled or willing.

"Yea, guess you should."

It was slightly disappointing to hear him say that she could go. Cora turned and was about to step on the bus when a hand stopped her. She glanced over her shoulder with a questioning look at Dylan. He gave her a quick kiss on the lips.

"Goodnight, babe. Get home safe... text me."

She was at a loss for words. That was so sweet and perfect and what she would have wanted him to do. Maybe the version of Dylan in her head was what Dylan was in reality. She could only nod – promising that she would – and got on the bus. For a late bus, it was fuller than she thought. While there were plenty of seats to sit and be alone, there were still five people on the bus. Cora made her way to a seat, alone. The stupidest smile was on her face as she watched the Boston lights and neon signs pass by as the bus headed towards downtown and her apartment.

She really did like Dylan.

Chapter Five

Abuela had returned home yesterday. Cora had been summoned to the family dinner, but luckily her phone had died and no one had been able to reach her all day. Hell, she didn't even know that the battery was dead until she got off of work and wondered why no one had texted her. Well, why Clarice and Dylan hadn't texted her back. Work had been non-stop, but it was approaching the semi-annual sale time of the year. So, it made sense.

She had gone home from Dylan's place and spent most of that night texting him. It was easier to flirt when he wasn't in the room beside her. Cora never thought that she was that shy, but maybe she was. If not, she didn't have another explanation for it. The worst part was that Dylan started to really open up more about who he was, while she just kept quiet.

Dylan never had any pets growing up and was an only child. He did know how to ride a horse and slap a puck around on the ice. He played hockey, but only ever on the makeshift rinks in the dead of winter with the neighborhood kids. He never even tried out for the school teams. And the reason that he was single was because his job used to make him travel a lot more, and none of his ex-girlfriends had wanted to deal with that. If that was the price to pay for dating Dylan, it wasn't take steep. Besides, maybe she could tag along sometimes and share a hotel room. They could see the sights together.

Meanwhile, she had spilled the beans to Clarice about Pad Thai and his apartment. She had debated for two minutes whether or not to tell her about the kiss and awkward moments, but Clarice was her best friend for a reason. She could be trusted with hearing these things and maybe she'd even have some advice for Cora. She had expected rapid-fire interrogation texts, or at least a phone call. Neither came. All she got was a couple emojis back and the promise to call her. Something was going on with Clarice, or rather, someone was going on Clarice.

Cora had tried not to let it get to her. So, having ran right into one of the busy seasons at work actually wasn't so bad. It had distracted her. That, and it gave her multiple excuses to get out of family dinners – not that she had actually needed any to get out of another dinner with abuela.

She plopped down on her couch and just deleted all her voicemails and texts from her mother, sister, brother-in-law... Her finger hovered over Dylan's message thread. They both agreed that they wanted another date but – yet again – they hadn't set a time or place right then. He said that his job might be sending him out of town for a trip, and now she knew how hard that must be on him. He was probably more worried about losing her over it just like he had his exes. Cora might have to wait another week to see him again, which was disappointing.

Her bank account had some spare change this week, even after the bills were paid. It gave her an idea to hit Clarice up. Hopefully, she'd be done playing with whatever man was around. Talking face-to-face was a lot faster than texting. Plus, sometimes she didn't always understand what Clarice was trying to text with all the emojis, and abbreviations, and slang.

Cora tapped the screen to call her best friend, but the worst possible thing happened. Her mother had called and, at the last second, the screen had changed, and she accepted the call.

"Hello? Hello? Coriara?" She could hear her mother's voice without even putting the phone next to her ear. "This is your mother. I know you're there. Pick up the phone."

Did she not realize that Cora had accidentally done that? Okay, so what were the chances that she could play it off as if her mother got the voicemail? With each second that ticked on, the odds got worse. Once her mother realized that she had answered the phone, there'd be hell to pay over "playing games" and making her wait so long to talk.

"Hey, mom." She tried not to sound like she was being tortured.

"You did not come to the family dinner to say goodbye to abuela. She was very upset, and we are upset with you too. You need to answer your phone. We are your family, and this was important. What if there was an emergency? How are we to reach you?"

Her mother was making it sound like dinner was an emergency. Everything was an emergency in her family. Ran out of adobo? An emergency. Couldn't reach the remote on the coffee table? An emergency. Not answering the phone? An emergency.

"My phone died, mom. It's not like I was doing it on purpose." This time. "Besides, I already saw abuela and gave her a hug. She probably didn't even notice that I wasn't there."

"Coriara, that is your abuela! Of course, she noticed that you weren't there."

Cora highly doubted that. There were too many of them in that house for abuela to know exactly who was there, who was hiding, and who just didn't show up. The one who noticed was her mother... who then probably asked her sister where she was... who probably then asked the rest of the family until everyone knew she had ditched. Again.

"I'm sorry, mom." Well, not really. Sorry that she had to sit through this lecture and phone call. Apologizing was the only thing that she could think of that might get her mom off her back, and off the phone.

"Well, your abuela's gone now so you can't see her." As if that would tear Cora up on the inside. "But we're having a family dinner tomorrow night. Your nephew, Diego, won his soccer game. You will be there, Coriara."

She started to use a date with Dylan as an excuse before she realized that would just keep her mother on the phone longer. She didn't want that. That and her cover could be blown if her mother tried to invite Dylan to dinner too. Then it was a rock and a hard place about what to do. If Cora did invite him and he went, her family would drive him insane and he'd go running for the hills. If she didn't, then she'd have to face her family alone and get bombarded with a new set of questions. More along the lines of *if* Dylan even existed at all.

"Fine, I'll be there." She caved.

"Great!" Cora could practically hear the smile on her mother's face. "I'll tell your sister that you'll get here early to help with the tamales. Can't wait to see you tomorrow. Adios!"

Her mother hung up before she could get a word in, but that was the plan. Cora didn't want to get there early much less help her sister with making the dinner. It was a punishment to be there longer and it was sneaky to force her into the kitchen. Clearly her mother was trying to say that she needed to learn how to cook. Any other day, maybe it would have bothered her. It just made her think of being able to cook one dinner for Dylan. She could try to impress him with her cultural treasure of tamales. Or she could just buy some Taco Bell and hide all the food wrappers. Yea, that might work better for the two of them.

Forced into family dinner again

She sent a text to Dylan. A little part of her was hoping that he'd remember their last family dinner and the um, conversation, they had then. While it had caught Cora off guard, it had been kind of exciting and fun. Besides, she needed to text something to Dylan so that he'd think of her. Why not something that was the truth?

89

It took him an hour to text back and, by then, Cora had already fallen asleep on the couch with an empty Chinese food container laying on the floor by her. She hadn't heard the ping of a text message go off because her snores had drowned it out. Instead, she found it the next morning when she went to use the bathroom and brought the phone for light entertainment while she did her business.

srry... good luck?

hey b heading outta town datenight next wekk mayb?

A sigh escaped, just like her hopes. She wasn't looking forward to waiting a week to see Dylan again. Seeing that he was going out of town for work, he probably wouldn't be able to text her as much either. So, it really was going to feel like he was gone, and she was still stuck here. Cora wished that she could escape, but there was a third – a threatening – text that reminded her that running was futile.

Mom said to pick you up for dinner. Be ready to go @ 5pm

Xiomara – less annoying known as Xo – was going to pick her up and Cora was going to stab herself with the pair of heels she was debating wearing tonight. Hopefully Tommy would be there too. It was a mystery how he had managed to tolerate – and love – her sister. Xo was a lot to handle and over the top. She was definitely the hot-blooded Latina that people thought of, and sort of Cora's opposite. Yet, Tommy had made things work for always ten years now and even had kids with Xo. On top of all that, he still tried to help buffer Cora from the family and save her ass a little. Tommy was a godsend and a saint and a gentleman.

And a huge Patriots fan.

Maybe he'd talk about the football team and what the stats were for this season. Actually, this family dinner might not be such a bad thing. She could get Tommy to talk about the football team then, on her next date, she could impress Dylan with all the information and stats that she knew. Then he'd know that she was the one for him – sexy fashionista and sport fan girl. Yea, she could probably do both.

Cora wanted to text her sister to make sure Tommy was going to be there but decided against it. Worst case scenario, he was at whatever soccer thing Diego had and was driving over separately. It meant that she'd be alone in the car with her sister for maybe fifteen minutes. It would be torture and the longest fifteen minutes of her life, but Cora thought that she might be able to survive that. She would just make sure to sit by Tommy at dinner and talk to him about all the sports stuff then.

She went to plug in her phone to charge – so her mother didn't lecture her on that later – then jumped into the shower. Her favorite cucumber melon body wash was almost gone. She'd have to make a mental note to pick more up at some point. Cora had a feeling that it was something that Dylan really liked, because he was always really close to her.

Cora decided to keep it simple. She grabbed a black tee and pulled on a pair of jeans. There really wasn't anything her family could say about this outfit – not that she was really looking for their approval. She did hope that downplaying her outfit might help her blend in more and get even more overlooked at dinner than normal.

At five o'clock, she was standing outside her apartment in her jean jacket with her hair pulled up into a ponytail. It had still taken her over an hour to get ready, but she needed to be on time for this. If she was just a minute late, Xo would lecture her the whole ride. If being a little inconvenienced like this would prevent that, then it was a small price to pay. Just like clockwork, the silver sedan pulled up and she climbed into the back with her cousin. Luckily, it wasn't going to be just Cora and her sister.

"Hey, Cora," Tommy greeted her. Diego was busy playing with a handheld video game. Xo had just rolled her eyes when she got into the car.

"Hey, thanks for picking me up." She wanted to keep it casually and nice. After all, she needed something from Tommy, and she didn't want anything from her sister.

"Well, mom said to so…"

Of course, her sister had to take a stab at her instead of just letting it go. It's not like they were inconvenienced by Cora. Her apartment was basically along the way. Normally, Cora would have pointed that out and took a stab back at her sister, but she was a girl on a mission. If she wanted Tommy, she had to play.

"So, Tommy, you're a Patriots fan… right?" She asked.

"Yea."

Xo groaned. "Don't get him started, Cora. I've heard all that I can about that stupid team today."

Well, shit. That threw a wrench into things. If she wanted to talk about football, she was going to have to do it away from Xo. If she brought it up now, it would probably just make her sister furious. Any other day, that might have been a fun plan to annoy her sister and enjoy the chaos. For now, Cora was resigned to stare out the window until they got to her parents' house.

There were a couple cars parked in the driveway when they showed up. It looked like they were the last to arrive, and Cora would probably get the blame for that. Xo and Diego started to walk in, but she hung back, hoping to get to talk to Tommy. If she could get the sports talk out of the way, then she could go hide somewhere until dinner was ready. But her father came around the corner and called him over. Cora had no choice but to wait until dinner and hope to snag a seat next to him so that she could get the scoop.

"Coriara, there you are!" Shit. She'd been spotted by her mother. Now there was no chance to just sneak off to one of the rooms and hide out until it was too late to help in the kitchen. Sighing, Cora gave up and followed after her mother. "I don't know why you're just standing out there. You must help make tamales with Xiomara. Don't you ever want to be able to feed your family? How can you expect to keep a husband if he starves?"

"Mom, I'm not married and I don't have kids yet." Maybe her mother was senile like abuela.

"Well, not with that kind of an attitude. Now go." Her mother gave her a push into the kitchen. "Put on an apron and help your sister."

Xo was already at work making the filling, so she tried to just hang back. Did they really want to risk illness or death by having Cora cook?

"Grab the corn husks from the pantry," Xo ordered. So, it was going to be like this – just like when they were kids. Xo would be the bossy older one, trying to tell her what to do.

Rolling her eyes, she went to grab the corn husks. In her mind, Cora kept repeating to herself that she needed Xo's husband. She needed Xo's husband. Bringing them over, she set the on the counter. That wasn't good enough though.

"Take them out and open them up. I can't put the filling in them if you leave them in the package. And also turn on the stove so the water will start boiling. I don't want to wait forever to steam these."

Cora fought hard to keep her mouth shut. She just had to do what her sister said and then it would all be over.

"What's wrong with you? Usually you say something."

Well, so much for getting away with keeping her mouth shut. Now she was going to have to talk and she was going to have to watch what she said. "It's just that I don't have much to say."

"Which isn't like you," she quipped back.

"Well, maybe I don't want to talk. Did you think of that?"

Xo rolled her eyes. "Even if you don't want to talk, you never just shut up and let me boss you around."

She had a point. "Well, maybe I'm just trying not to set mom off. Getting in a fight with you is just going to send her after me with another wave of guilt trips. Did you know that I upset abuela because I wasn't here the other day to say goodbye?"

"No." Xo grabbed one of the corn husks that Cora pulled out and started to fill it. "Abuela never mentioned your name. Like, she totally should have been talking about you. You did drop that huge bomb on everyone."

Cora knew what she meant but tried to play the fool. "What bomb?"

Her sister set down the tamale and turned to face her, hands on her hips. "That you got some boyfriend? Like, is that true and why haven't we met him?"

"Yes, Coriara, why haven't we met this boy?"

She turned around to see her mother walk into the kitchen. This was either a set-up where they were working together or her mother was micro-managing again and trying to rush them along. There was a slim chance that she could have distracted Xo with some fashion or celebrity gossip but there was no way to throw off her mother. Cora had a whole childhood of failed attempts. There was no choice but to fess up.

"First, I *do* have a boyfriend and his name is Dylan," she started. Her mother scoffed, probably disappointed that Dylan didn't sound like a Hispanic name. "We just started dating a couple weeks ago and I just thought that it was too soon to bring him around here."

"A couple weeks?" Her mother looked like her eyes were going to pop out of her head. "Coriara, you are practically married. We should have met him by now! You call him and tell him to come to dinner right now."

She groaned. This was exactly why Dylan would never come to family dinners. There was no way he'd stick around with her mother being like this. How Tommy dealt with it, she'd never know. "He's out of town this week for work, mom."

"Working out of town? Either he's got some fancy job or he's cheating on you, Cora." Her sister came out of nowhere with that.

"He's not cheating on me."

"Then what does he do?" Cora should have expected this question, but it didn't change the fact that she hadn't asked Dylan. So, when she shrugged, her sister cursed in Spanish and then her mother started in on a lecture about ladylike behavior.

"Coriara, you must ask him what he does. You need to protect your man from these loose women." Her mother flicked her hand in the air at "loose women".

They didn't know Dylan like she did, and they didn't know how he was around her. Cora could say all that she wanted to prove them wrong about this out-of-town work trip, but nothing she said was going to change their opinions.

"I'll do that, mom." Yea, like eventually. Her mother and sister probably wanted answers right now and expected Cora to bust out her phone and demand them from him. "Shouldn't we finish making the tamales? I bet everyone's hungry."

Her mother narrowed her eyes at Cora. "Yes, they are hungry. Okay, back to work."

Cora breathed a sigh of relief when her mother left. Her sister, though, still remained and she could see the questioning look on Xo's face. At least with her sister, she could ignore her. It wouldn't be as fun as shooting off her mouth like she could have done before, but it would still get under her sister's skin and that would make it worth it.

She took out all the husks, laying them flat, and then decided to grab a spoon. Watching Xo, she tried to mimic how her sister stuffed them. It had to be killing Xo on the inside that she was being ignored, but her sister didn't say anything. They got all the corn husks stuffed and then laid them on the steamer rack in the pot to cook. Cora whipped off that apron and was out of the kitchen before her sister could set the lid on the pot. She needed to find Tommy and get down to business.

Tommy and her father were sitting out in the backyard with beers in their hands. Her father told a joke that got Tommy laughing, which made her father look pleased. Her father didn't always have a good sense of humor. Cora wondered if he even knew what a joke was, let alone what a good joke was. When she took a seat with them at the picnic table, the joking and laughs died down. It felt awkward for Cora, like she had walked into a "boys only" club meeting.

"Hey, so what you guys talking about?" Maybe asking that would alleviate some of the tension. If she was included, then it shouldn't be awkward. Right?

"Nothing, Coriara. Just funny man stuff."

Tommy took a swig of his beer and actually tried to include her. "So, how'd things go in the kitchen with the tamales? Are we eating tonight?"

That last bit got her father laughing. Cora knew that he meant it all in good fun, but her father's reaction was a bit depressing. The family really did think that she couldn't cook, or that her food would either burn down the house or kill them all.

"It actually wasn't that bad. Xo did most of the work, so you all are safe to eat dinner," she tried to joke back. "Maybe one of you can talk mom out of making me help with dinner next time."

"But then how you cook for your husband?" Her father looked at her like she said something confusing. Really, though, her parents needed to stop calling Dylan her husband or else it would get into her head and then *that* would be an awkward conversation.

"One, papa, he's not my husband. He's just a boy I'm dating and, no, I'm not inviting him over because mom would scare him away. Two, Dylan's a really good cook. He invited me over to his place for dinner and made Pad Thai. He said it was Thai food, but it just looked like Chinese food to me."

"Ah." Her father nodded his head, like he just had a revelation and figured it all out now. Maybe he would end up being the most logical and sane one of her family – minus Tommy, of course. "He's gay and likes the men."

Oh father, I had such high hopes for you!

"I don't think Cora is trying to tell you that he's gay. Some men live alone and need to learn how to cook. Some men also learn to cook to impress the ladies."

98

Tommy stepped in to explain, slowly, to her father. "So, think of it as him being a man that could take care of Cora."

"Oh, yes. Well, that's good then."

Cora mouthed to her brother-in-law a thank you. It was just annoying that neither of her parents would just take her word on things. Seeing as her sister sided a lot with her mother, it made talking about things a lot harder. She definitely appreciated Tommy and his help.

"So, is there anything going on with the Patriots? Like, is there a game coming up or did they do something good in their last one?" She wanted to get her answers and hide before another round of interrogations could start.

This time it was Tommy that laughed.

"What?" Cora didn't think that she had said anything wrong.

"Sounds like this Dylan is a Patriots fan and little Cora wants to pretend that she is too," he teased.

Well, he wasn't wrong.

"No, I just want to know some things so that I don't look stupid if he wants to talk about it." And to impress him and get him thinking that they were a perfect match because she was also a Patriots fan.

"Well, the Patriots have a pass this week." Tommy took another swig of his beer. "Plus, their last game was bad. Like, really bad. No one is going to want to talk about that."

So – what she was hearing – there was no point in coming to this family dinner because there was nothing going on with the Patriots. Just like with her relationship. Cora groaned and got up. She was going to head into the house and hide from her family in some room again. Behind her, she could hear Tommy chuckle.

"Guess you have to come to the next family dinner, Cora. We'll tell you all the good stuff then!"

Everyone was in the living room, talking about Diego and the soccer game. Seeing that Cora hadn't seen it – much less been told about it – there was no point in hanging around with all her cousins and sisters. She headed back to her old room and found a place to hide between the bed, wall, and night stand. It felt lonely being here. It would have been nice if her family talked to her about other things than Dylan. She was a person with likes and hobbies. She was more than just some guy. And all the talk about Dylan just made her miss him.

Miss u

She sent the message, hoping for a quick reply. He was probably traveling to wherever. Hopefully when he got to a safe spot, Dylan would see the message and smile. That would make her happy – knowing that she had put a smile on his face. It would be even better to know that it wasn't because she had said or done something stupid and he laughed at her. This would be genuine.

Her mother eventually came around to announce that dinner was done. Apparently, there were some of her cousins that wanted to stay outside and play. They were bribed inside with the promise of flan.

Cora got up from her hiding spot and made her way to the dining room table. Fortunately, she had talked to

Tommy already because there wasn't a free seat near him. Cora was stuck with her younger – and more annoying – cousins. The plate of tamales got passed around and Cora was happy to see that they actually turned out looking legit, and good. Yea, she knew that Xo really should take the credit because she basically had put them altogether. It still made Cora feel good to know that she had helped a little – and they didn't taste bad at all!

She was mostly ignored at dinner. Everyone had switched topics and were talking about the soccer game and how well Diego had played. Apparently, he was pretty good, and the school was thinking about letting him move up to varsity next year instead of the junior team. It was all great news, but it didn't interest Cora. She killed time on her phone until dinner was over and it was time to clean up. Most of her sisters were packing up the cousins to take home for bed. Basically, that left Xo and her to clean up. Lucky them!

It went by quickly and Tommy claimed to have an early work meeting, so they were out the door fast. The drive back to Cora's apartment was quiet this time. Maybe her sister got her fill of information or maybe Xo knew that any more questions tonight would be ignored.

"It was great that you could make it to dinner tonight," Tommy said as she got out. "If you ever need a ride, text Xo and we'd gladly pick you up."

It was either a nice offer or Tommy had been brainwashed into guilt tripping her, like the rest of the family. Seeing as he had saved her ass a couple times tonight, she decided that he was just trying to be nice.

"I'll keep that in mind. Get home safe!" She called back to them as she climbed up the front stairs.

Slipping inside her building, she was greeted with heat and it made her drowsy after filling her tummy. The stairs probably would be the best option. It would help burn some of the calories that she put into her mouth and the exercise to get rid of some these extra curves. The stairs could make her sexy for Dylan... Cora hit the elevator call button.

There still was no reply from Dylan. It made Cora feel a little... upset? She wasn't sure of the exact word to describe these feelings. She did know that a glass of wine would help, and there just happened to be some left in a bottle from when Clarice spent the night last month.

Miss U bad
Need U bad

Cora smiled at his texts. He missed her too! Her mind drifted a little to what her mother said at dinner. Dylan wouldn't be missing her if he was cheating. It kind of reassured her that Cora was the only one. This was real.

Wish you were here & not working

She sent the text, not even thinking to play it cool and not be so clingy. She got up and went to top off her second glass of wine, not expecting anything more from Dylan tonight. Halfway to the kitchen, her phone dinged.

Wanna CU

send pix

Pix? What the hell was that and why did he want her to send them?

Send me urs n I'll give ya a surprise

Cora stared at the screen, still a little confused. Maybe it was the wine; maybe it wasn't. What could he want her to send that he could also give her? ... oh, pix were photos!

She opened up the camera app and tried to take a cute selfie. The first two attempts – her eyes were closed and she looked drunk. Then there were a bunch where her finger slipped over the lens. It took a while before Cora thought one was good enough to send him. Maybe tomorrow she wouldn't think that, but tonight it was the perfect selfie.

No a pix
Wanna c that body ;)

Her eyes tried to focus on the words. So, a selfie wasn't a pix? He wanted to see her body too... but, like, how? Cora texted him back to ask what he meant.

show me BooBs

Oh... boobs. Her mind had a thought, for a second, but it was gone. Cora was on her second refill of her second glass of wine, which if someone really wanted to do the math meant that she was drinking her third glass of wine. And, for an occasionally drinker, it meant that Cora was pretty tipsy. But it also meant that now she understood what Dylan wanted with these pix.

A tee shirt wasn't too revealing, and it wasn't the kind of top that showed off her boobs. Boobs hadn't been a thought when she was trying to come up with an outfit for dinner. Although, maybe it should have been. Xo and her older cousins all liked dressing that way. Perhaps she should take a page out of their boobie book.

It meant the shirt had to go then. If Dylan wanted boobs, there was no way around it. But it meant setting down the glass of wine and her phone for a minute. Cora tried to pull off her shirt but it someone got stuck on her head. She tried to pull it off harder but lost her balance and fell off the couch. It was the stupidest thing and she probably looked like a mess, but it didn't matter. Cora was laughing at herself, but the shirt was finally off! She held the phone under her nose to make sure that her boobs were in the photo. It was kind of hard for her to tell if her boobs were there at all because she had a pink lacy bra on, and her drunk eyes just saw pink skin everywhere.

I want those

Dylan texted back almost immediately. The fact that he said that he wanted her had put a smile on her face. He really, really did like her!

shoe me more babe

take it of

She read his texts, twice. She may have been tipsy, but she wasn't so sure that Dylan was making sense. He wanted her to take it off? Take what off? She couldn't take off her skin.

I can' t take it off silly

But almost immediately, he set a text back.

pls u so hot... wanna c all u
babe Im so hard
show me all u
send me nude
I'll give u me if ur a good girl

His texts had come one right after another. Each one made her feel something different. Dylan had called her hot, and that one photo had made him aroused. Like, he really wanted. She tried not to get emotional and choked up as she took another sip of her wine. He wanted to see all of her! He wasn't turned off at all by how she looked. He wanted more! And Cora wanted to be a good girl for him.

She set down the glass of wine and phone again. Her mind was focused on one thing, one goal. Clumsily, her hands tried to unclasp the back of her bra, but it seemed like nothing was working to get it to open up. If only Dylan was here! He'd be able to get it open so fast and then she could take that photo to send him. Yea, if he was here then he could take the photo for her and it would probably look better. Cora bet that photo would make him happier than any she could take herself.

The bra wasn't letting go.

"Fuck this!"

Cora shoved it down, so it hung around her waist. The cool air of her apartment tickled her tits, making her giggle. Her giggling made her think of Dylan's laugh. Oh, he was just going to love these. She couldn't help but get distracted by her own boobs and ended up playing with them. That was until she remembered why she needed to get free of that bra in the first place.

Biting her bottom lip, she tried hard to focus on what she was doing. It was getting harder and harder to focus on what she was doing. Cora knew that she wanted this photo to look the best, but her boobs wouldn't play nice and kept trying to run away. She tried to hold them together with one arm while she took the photo. They ended up looking squished together and huge. But was it good enough for Dylan? Maybe he couldn't see enough. Maybe she should take one without holding them together. Cora held the phone further away so that she could get her whole top half in the photo.

She flipped back and forth between the photos, unable to tell which one looked better. Cora couldn't decide. Maybe she should just send both and then Dylan could pick which one he wanted. Yea, she'd send both... more was better... Dylan would like her boobs...

Her mind felt in a fog when she finally woke up. Looking around, this wasn't her bedroom. Nothing was making sense.

"Ugh, why am I on the floor?" She groaned, getting up.

And why was her bra shoved down around her waist? The air caused her to shiver and she felt the skin on her chest tingle. Cora grabbed the bra and pulled it back, locking her boobs back up. And where was her shirt? She couldn't find it until she walked around the couch and saw it back there. She pulled it on, wondering what the hell had happened last night. She had never gotten this crazy before. This was just plain weird.

Cora found her phone on the floor and picked up. There were text message notifications from Dylan and one missed call from him. She opened the chat window first and immediately tossed the phone away when she saw what was there.

"No, no, no..." She kept shaking her head. There was no way that she saw what she thought that she saw. There just was no way! Dylan didn't... because he wouldn't... and she hadn't...

Swallowing hard, Cora tried to build up enough courage to look at the messages again. The scariest part was thinking that the photo she saw was really what she saw. And if it was, it was just a photo. What harm was there from a photo? She was being ridiculous. Cora unlocked her phone and looked at the messages Dylan must have sent after she passed out.

open ur legs
show me ur wet

Between the texts, there was a photo. It made her stop breathing. Cora had nothing to judge it by other than Dylan's hand, but it looked huge. It looked thick and veiny and wow... Why would he send this? The tip was darkened like he had been... oh, god.

can u handle this?
u want it babe

Cora couldn't get pass that dick pic, though. It was a big distraction that took up almost the whole screen. Seeing it just made a million things run through her mind. One, she couldn't believe that Dylan had sent her *that*. Two, she wasn't sure how she felt about this now that she wasn't drunk – well, tipsy, because she didn't think that she actually got drunk.

A thought crossed her mind – had he been masturbating to her photos? Cora had no idea how she felt about that. But scrolling back up to re-read the whole conversation made her feel sick to her stomach. What had truly made her feel sick was seeing her boobs staring back at her. Cora never thought that she'd ever be the type to send that kind of photos. Yet, she had.

She felt disgraced and dirty. Who was she? Cora didn't know if she knew anymore. She tried to tell herself that she was just overreacting. After all, Clarice must have sent tons of these kind of photos. Hell, loads of girls probably sent full nudes or worse. Cora shuddered. Her mind didn't want to think about what "worse" could possibly be.

Cora deleted the photos out of the chat that were of her. All three of them. She didn't want to see them, and she didn't want proof on her phone that she had done anything. Right now, she couldn't accept what she had done. All she felt was shame and regret.

But she saved Dylan's dick photo to her phone.

Just in case.

Actually, she didn't know why she did that. It wasn't like she'd use his photo to masturbate like Dylan had done with hers. She wasn't even sure that she wanted to look at it. It was his dick for crying out loud! He shouldn't have sent that to her at all. Then again, she shouldn't have sent him that photo of her boobs either. Some might consider his photo a trophy, but Cora wasn't one of them. As long as no one else saw her boobs, she'd be happy with that. The fear that he might send it to someone else or show someone else was too much to handle and she didn't even want to think about it.

What she needed to do was shower and get her mind out of the haze so that she could think again. What day was it anyways? The last thing she needed was for it to be a work day, because that would probably mean that she was already running late. Knowing her luck, the boss would give her another citation for being late or just fire her. It was too early to bet on Dylan being her sugar daddy and, after that dick pic, she wasn't sure how she really felt about this relationship. Cora couldn't afford to lose her job right now.

Her phone said that it was Wednesday. That meant work. Luckily, it was still early enough for her to grab a quick shower and get to work. Although, Cora was going to have to cough up the cash for an Uber. It would take too long to get there on a bus making all the scheduled stops and there was probably no convincing of the bus driver to get them to pass up stops along the way. That would probably incite a riot.

Cora tossed her phone on to charge and hopped into the shower. She knew that her hair was just going to be a mess today when she got out of the shower. She told herself that it was fine because she really had no one to impress. Dylan was out of town and she really didn't think that she should be worrying about other guys. Right now, she was dating him, and they were basically boyfriend and girlfriend – just without having that talk. While there was practically zero percent change of another guy flirting with her and trying to ask her out, Cora was mostly sure that she'd turn them down because of Dylan. That's not to say that she wouldn't take their number if they gave it to her. Maybe she'd give it to Clarice or keep it just in case Dylan realized that he could do better than her.

There were plenty of Uber drivers on the road when she opened her app. One showed up within a couple minutes. Climbing in, she was a little disappointed that it was a woman driving. Guess that hypothetical scenario about meeting a guy and getting his phone number was just not meant to be. And why should she even want it to? Dylan made her feel wanted enough.

Despite every single wish and prayer Cora tossed up along the way, the store was still standing when the Uber pulled up. She gave the driver a smile and promised to tip later, as she got out of the car. Honestly, she wasn't sure if she would tip. That was extra money and Cora could barely afford to come to work. The whole system was broken. She should be getting paid to stay home instead and do nothing. It was ridiculous that it cost money to make money.

Two of the Plastics were sitting in the breakroom, talking about the sales, when she came in to clock-in for the day. She overheard Gucci and Armani but knew better than to ask where and what the sales were about. Although it was always her dream to have a real Gucci bag and a sale would be the only way to make it happen – forgetting that she was basically broke. And because they were gossiping about the sales and what next year's fashion trends might be, she slipped through unnoticed.

Cora just turned on the light to her register when she heard her phone ding. That needed to go on vibrate before the boss came by and caught her with a phone. If she was one of the Plastics, it probably wouldn't be a problem, but she wasn't one of the chosen few. She slipped her hand into her pocket and flipped the little switch to vibrate mode. But then curiosity got the better of her. Who texted her and what did it say?

U like?

It was a text from Dylan, and she knew what he was asking about. He was probably wondering a lot of things after last night. She had passed out without texting him back. Maybe he thought that it was a rejection or that Cora was still going to town on her lady parts. It made sense that he would ask what she thought of the photo.

111

There was really only two ways to answer that – a yes or a no. It was more than just asking about a photo. If Cora said that she didn't like it, it was probably the end of whatever they had going on. Honestly, there really was no choice. She was trapped into the answer and whatever may come from it.

Yea

A text came back almost immediately. It was just a smiley face emoji, but it was enough to make her uneasy. It was the answer that Dylan wanted, but she wasn't so sure that it was the right thing to do. Cora wished that she didn't have to think about that photo and wished that he would just let it die.

She hid her phone and got back to work. There was already a woman loading her items onto the register's conveyor belt. One thing that would be a distraction from dicks was work. Today, Cora would be the best cashier this store had ever seen. She'd put it all into her job today.

Things changed on Cora's lunchbreak. She sat down to eat the leftovers her mother sent home and surf the internet when a text message popped up. This time, it was Clarice. If it had been Dylan or her family, she probably would have ignored it. It had been days since she talked to her best friend. It was so unlike Clarice to just vanish like this, so – Cora assumed – whoever had her best friend's attention was definitely a big deal. That or there was some family thing going on and, unlike her own family, it probably was a real emergency type thing.

Sorry its been a year. Dad was in hospital. Work accident. What I miss?

Clarice's dad worked for a roofing company, so a workplace accident was major. There were probably broken bones, at least. It must have been terrifying for her dad, and to get that call that he was in the hospital... Cora felt for her best friend. What was going on in her life was nothing compared to what Clarice had been dealing with. And here she had thought that Clarice was off having some fling with a guy all week.

Srry about your dad. He gonna be ok?

First things, first.

Yea. No broken bones but he hurt his leg bad. Gotta use crutches now. So this guy you seeing...?

Well, Cora did try not to make it about her right away but Clarice wanted to know. Honestly, she probably wanted a distraction from thinking that he dad got lucky and it wasn't something a lot worse. As far as distractions, Dylan was a complete distraction. It just was... where to start?

Yea, 2nd date he made me Pad Thai. It was like Chinese food tho. He got really flirty, pinned me in kitchen to kiss me

Clarice sent the WOW emoji.

Gurl he likes u bad! He good kisser?

It wasn't really a question if he was a good kisser or not. In her opinion, it was a nice kiss and probably something that she would want to happen again. The whole thing was just about *how* he kissed her. It was a lot more forward than she expected. Knowing what Clarice was going through now, it didn't seem like something that she should really bring up. It didn't feel like it would be right to have their normal gossiping while her dad was hurt like that. Besides, everything had turned out alright after that. So, it didn't seem like talking about it was important anymore. There was something else that Cora would rather talk about, even though she'd rather forget it ever happened.

Dylan can def kiss

When ya seeing him again?

Dunno. He's working outta town atm

But ya still talkin, right?

This was it. This was where she could bring up the photo or leave it out like it never happened. It wasn't like Clarice would really ever find out any other way that he had sent a dick pic. If she ever did though, she would probably feel incredibly hurt that Cora hadn't told her and that was something that she didn't want to. Besides, Clarice was the only one that she could talk to about it and maybe she could help Cora process all the thoughts and feelings that she was having.

Yea... we kinda flirty sexy last night. I got drunk off that wine you left behind.

As if that was a legit excuse. Cora was hoping that if her best friend knew she was drunk that her opinions on what Cora did might be more sugar-coated.

So ya sexted?

Um, no... he asked for pix

There was a long pause. It seemed like Clarice didn't know what to say. She knew that Cora had never sent nudes before because it was something that they had talked about in the past. She also knew that Cora had no idea what a sexy photo looked like, let alone how to take them to lure in a guy.

I didn't send one... he did tho

It was a lie – a white lie, she told herself. There was no point in Clarice knowing that she sent a topless photo. The only thing that photo did was make her uneasy about what Dylan could be using it for or who he could be showing it to. Did he worry about the same thing? Did Dylan wonder if she'd be showing his dick around? Part of her reasoned that he was just that cocky not to care, and he might actually be bold enough to ask what they said about the size and girth of it.

Was it sick?

No, looked fine

No, like how big?

Um, big?

Cora, was it huge or like normal...

Well, it looks bigger than my ex's

That's good... rite?

The whole dick pic thing didn't seem to surprise Clarice. It didn't seem like it really was that big of a deal. Maybe this was all just a normal part of dating and she was blowing it out of proportions just because it's never happened to her before. Cora was finding out that there were a lot of things that she was running into for the first time – like getting cheesy pick-up lines in a grocery store's meat section.

There was one way to answer all of Clarice's questions. She had already rationalized that Dylan wouldn't care. The fear was that maybe Clarice would take more interest in her man than she should. If it came down to a choice between Cora or Clarice, Clarice had her completely beat in the looks and experience department. She was the better match for Dylan. But did Cora really believe that her best friend would steal her boyfriend? Of course not. At least, when she was being logical.

Cora opened up her chat log with Dylan and forwarded the photo. It was just easier that way. Clarice would see it any moment and have all her questions answered. Maybe she'd even be able to tell Cora if it was a good dick or something that she should have laughed at. Maybe it was actually really small, and Dylan was just over compensating for it with the over-the-top personality and flirty advances.

Wow

That one word was kind of all that she needed to hear. Dylan was impressive and definitely not compensating. It was Clarice's next text that really made her wonder about things.

Are you gonna be ok with that? The sex?

They hadn't talked much about Cora's sex life. Partly because it seemed to take forever before she had one with her ex-boyfriend, and then it seemed a little too personal and inappropriate to talk about. For Clarice, she lost interest because the sex scoop was boring. Meanwhile, she was out enjoying different men and different positions. Things were never the same every time they talked. That and she knew Cora hadn't been

117

happy with the sex near the end of her last relationship. Cora even admitted that it was boring, and she tried to get out of doing it as much as possible. Sex wasn't fun anymore and that connection had disappeared.

Yea? I mean, it's too soon for sex

But he sent a dick pic... he thinkin about it

Maybe it was just a friendly warning or maybe it was supposed to be a question and Clarice forgot to add the question mark symbol at the end. She waited for Clarice to say something else – anything else – because she didn't know what to say to that. But she never did. At least, Cora didn't know if she said anything else because her lunchbreak was done, and she was being forced to go back out into that horrible place. She pocketed her phone and sucked it up.

Chapter Six

When she got off work, there were two text messages waiting for her from Dylan.

Cummin back tomorrow
Wanna go out Friday nite?

Friday night. The real, legit date night of date nights. Dylan was actually going to take her out and show her off as his girl. And he had said they'd be going out and it wasn't something like spending the night in, watching Netflix or something. This was going to be a real, major date. Those two little texts were getting her nerves going.

Friday night wasn't her guaranteed day off. That was Thursday. That was why their other dates happened then. There was no way in hell that one of the Plastics would switch shifts with her. Unless it benefited them, they wouldn't agree to anything. Cora would need to double check the schedule but – if she was working – she was probably going to need to just call in sick that day. There was no way that she could leave it to chance or just go on their date after her shift. Cora needed time to get properly ready for a date and she didn't want to be sweaty or smelling like a cheap department store.

Yes :)

It wouldn't give her much time to obsess over this date, seeing as it was only a couple days away. Her fingers were itching to ask what Dylan had in mind this time, but she stashed the phone in her pocket instead. It could be a surprise. The two previous dates had seen planned ones where Cora knew what they were doing and even were Dylan asked if the dates were okay. This could be something completely new and a complete surprise to Cora. The only downside was that she probably wouldn't know what to wear. For that, she'd at least need a hint.

Cora wasn't sure why he was springing for cab fare. They could easily have taken a bus – or two – and gotten here within an hour or so. Okay, maybe it didn't make much sense to do that. Dylan had actually dressed up. Then again, so had she. Maybe it was better that they took a cab instead of risking stains and annoying commuters on the bus. This date was kind of a big deal – this was the third one. This was the one that would make their relationship Facebook official. They had made it this far, so putting a label on it was long overdue.

The cab pulled up to the corner of Tremont and Waltham Streets. On the corner was a little restaurant and had to be the place that they were going. It didn't look super fancy, but it wasn't a dump either. Glancing down at her dress, she realized that she had chosen the right one to wear. It wasn't too casual and seemed to fit in with what the rest of the crowd was wearing. Dylan's khaki pants and polo were the gold standard anywhere, so an outfit must have been a small thought to him.

Dylan got out and hurried to the other side where he extended a hand to help her out of the cab. His fingers slipped between hers as they headed to the door. Like a gentleman, he got the door and held it open for her.

"Welcome to Tawney's. Table for two?" The woman at the podium asked them.

He nodded. "I made a reservation. It should be under Haggerty."

Having grabbed two menus, the woman paused and glanced down at her list. "Ah, yes, we do have a reservation for you. You requested a table near the window."

Table near the window? Cora glanced his way but he was completely oblivious. If they were seated by the window, then anyone walking along the street could glance inside and see them. It made her stomach flip. Dylan really wanted to show her off. It wasn't just all in her head.

Dylan pulled out her chair for her before taking a seat across from her at the table. The woman set their menus down in front of them and let them know that their waiter would be around momentarily to take their order. Having never been here before, Cora was going to need more than a moment to look over the menu and figure out what she wanted to eat. Dylan was her boyfriend now and not just an opportunity for free food. She needed to start thinking about how much was acceptable for a date because she didn't want to take advantage of him and order the most expensive thing.

"What looks good to you?"

Cora glanced up from the menu. There was a certain look in his eye that made her believe it wasn't a question solely based on the menu card in her hand. It was just starting to feel emotionally acceptable to allow herself to take a page out of his book and comment that he looked good to her. Cora had already told him in the cab when he picked her up, but maybe he wanted to hear it again. Maybe it meant something more to hear it in a nicer place, like this, instead of outside her apartment building on the street. Then again, why stroke his ego any more? Dylan knew that he looked good. The woman that seated them was giving him the look-over and it wouldn't be a surprise if her phone number came written down on the check.

Maybe next time she would take the bait and it would be easier to tell her boyfriend all those cutesy things. "The boeuf à la bourguignonne caught my eye."

Just the boeuf à la bourguignonne? She could almost hear him asking that. It was hard to play the flirty game when she was up against a master. Maybe if she had more time to think or if Clarice had been around to act out scenarios to give her quick comebacks.

"You said that in flawless Italian," he commented. The smile on his face was huge, even though he was completely wrong. Cora only knew Spanish – if that could be considered a foreign language for her – but she knew that what she said was actually supposed to be French. "I'm going with the second-best thing in this place – Wagyu Denver Steak."

Don't do it. Don't do it.

"What's the first?" For a second, she thought it might have actually been what she decided to order, but he started to smirk and she knew that wasn't the case. Dylan nodded towards her. It was cheesy, but at the same time it had her blushing and feeling like a love-struck puppy. The idea that Dylan thought she was the best thing in the place was definitely a great thing to hear. It somehow validated parts of her life that he never even touched – like things with her ex-boyfriend and family. It almost didn't matter if it was cheesy. Someone validated her.

"Well, I think you're pretty great yourself, handsome." It probably sounded just as cheesy.

In all actuality, Dylan seemed to almost not acknowledge it. He probably got called handsome all the time with a face like that. He probably had hundreds of girls, and girlfriends, tell him he was good looking. Or maybe he was so full of himself that he already was operating under the assumption that he was god's gift to women – maybe even to mankind too. Cora wanted to think that it was none of that. That Dylan could just feel it from her; that he just knew how she felt.

The waiter came back, and he ordered for them both, including a bottle of red wine that Cora wasn't sure needed to be added. Let's just say that red wine wasn't her cup of tea when she went for wines. Her sweet tooth did get the better of her and drew her more to the whites. That and there was this outrageously horrible accident that involved two glasses of red wine and a borrowed shirt from her sister... who would never let it go.

The waiter had already poured her glass and went to Dylan's by the time her stroll down memory lane was over. She had missed whatever ramblings about the selection and missed the opportunity to turn the glass of wine down. Cora really didn't care that she missed out on hearing if it was a good year for grapes in the south of France or Northern Italy or the water temperatures of Bermuda where it was sourced from the spring.

Cora reached for the glass to take a sip. This really was a bit too much, and the worst part was the wine. Either it was some shitty stuff or too rich for her tastes to comprehend. She set it back down on the table and vowed that she wouldn't touch it again tonight. Hopefully, the waiter would bring out some water for the table as well and she could drink that instead.

"So how was your work trip?" She asked, trying to make small talk. They actually hadn't talked about that and Cora was actually curious how it had gone. She was also curious about what he did for work after her family brought it up.

He shrugged. "It went okay."

Instead of saying more, Dylan took a sip of the wine and commented on how good it was. Clearly, they had different tastes. That seemed to extend to conversation too. She did wonder though if she asked him directly whether or not he would come out and say what he does. Like her brother-in-law always said with his sports reference – you miss a hundred percent of the shots you never take.

"I don't think you've ever told me," She knew that he didn't, "but what do you do for work?"

Dylan took another sip of his wine and actually looked like he was debating whether or not to tell her. Or maybe he was deciding on how much to tell her. "I work in accounting."

Accounting? How did that translate to having to work out of town?

"And your job sent you out of town? I thought accountants just sat at desks all day in some dark cubicle."

He laughed. "Normally yes. Let's just say that I do audits on places and need to be on-site for that."

Well, that made sense she guessed. There really was no point in asking for more details. Dylan seemed to be closed-lipped about this, just like he was with everything else. The only thing that he wasn't was about sex, it seemed. Well, that wasn't true. They actually hadn't talked about sex, he just got really flirty and sexual in his texts.

"So, did you do anything else naughty while I was gone?" There was a devilish look in his eye when he asked that. It was probably safe to assume that he was thinking about the topless photo that she sent, and probably assuming that Cora was a bit of a wild child.

"No." She shook her head slightly. Then the question popped in her mind. Did Dylan do anything else naughty while he was gone? Did he send his dick pic to anyone else? The question was going to drive her insane but, luckily, he had opened the conversation up to where she could find out. "Did you?"

Dylan smirked. "Maybe."

That definitely wasn't the answer that Cora wanted to hear. She didn't want to think about what he might have been doing or with whom. It fed into the fear that her family mentioned – maybe Dylan was cheating on her with someone else. Hell, maybe she was the mistress and didn't know it.

"Would you really be with someone else behind my back?" She didn't want to sound needy or clingy, but that was all that question was. There was no way around it.

He reached across the table and held her hand. "I wouldn't do that."

And she wanted to believe him. She really did and he did sound sincere. The waiter brought out their plates of food and Dylan had to take his hand back to eat. That little gesture had meant a lot and Cora could immediately feel it missing.

She watched as he cut off a piece of steak and took a bite, so she decided to follow suit. They are in silence for a few minutes before Dylan thought to say something.

"How is it?"

"It's good. Would you like to try a bite?" Usually she wouldn't have offered but there wasn't a guarantee that they'd be back here again. What harm was there in sharing?

He shook his head. "No, that's okay. Just as long as you're enjoying it, that's all that matters."

Dylan took his wine glass and held it out towards Cora. It took her a moment to realize that he was trying to say a toast, which he was really too late for. It didn't stop her from taking her glass and gently clinking it against his. It put a smile on his face, which was all she needed.

The rest of the meal went by quietly, except for when Dylan kept encouraging her to enjoy the "amazing" wine. Cora finished her glass, just so that she didn't insult him. When the check came, he kept it far from her, like she was going to peek or try to steal the bill to pay. Guess he hadn't figured out that she broke, which may not have been a bad thing. When he got up to go pay the check, Cora glanced at her phone. There were a couple texts from her family but – again – no real emergencies. There was one from Clarice, wishing her an awesome date.

"Shall we go?" Dylan asked when he got back to the table.

Cora nodded and took his offered hand. He helped her up and kept her hand in his as they headed towards the door. The city was busy tonight, but it was to be expected on a Friday. They had just stepped outside the restaurant and were standing in the middle of the sidewalk. Cora glanced up at him, expecting him to give her some idea of what was going to happen. Like, shouldn't they get a cab? Or were they going out dancing or to see some movie?

"So, what now?" Cora asked, hoping that she didn't come off as demanding. Really, dinner had been great and probably cost him a lot of money. She wasn't trying to use him and hoped it didn't seem that way.

He smiled, softly, down at her. "How about we go to your place?"

Her place? Her place was a mess right now. Even if it was clean, it was a dump compared to his. She had no idea why Dylan would ever want to go there. Although, her place was closer than his. Maybe that had something to do with it. Maybe they'd go back to her place and watch a movie or something. There was a Redbox around the corner in the bodega.

"Okay."

Dylan hailed a cab and opened the door for her to get in when one pulled up to the curb. He walked around and slide into the backseat with her as Cora told the driver her address. The whole way back to her place, Dylan sat close. He held her hand and kept it resting on his leg. He seemed a little different tonight, but in a good way. He seemed like he was starting to be the man of her dreams, and she was starting to feel like a princess.

When they got to her apartment, he was right there to open her door. Leaning back into the cab's window, he paid the driver before following her up the front steps of the apartment building. Cora was a little afraid to look at him. She didn't want to see his nose turned up and the disgust on his face of having to come to a place like this.

"I'm sorry it's not as nice your place." She felt like she had to apologize for something that she didn't know was going to be a problem or an embarrassment this morning.

"Don't worry, babe."

But she was worrying. While her building had a working elevator, that was all that it had going for it. Dylan might have been fine with the apartment building so far, but he hadn't seen her apartment yet. That mess might change his mind. She needed to warn him. If he was mentally prepared for a warzone, then maybe he wouldn't leave running.

"I have to warn you that it's a mess. I didn't know that we'd be coming back here." Her fingers fumbled with getting the key into the lock.

"Babe, I said not to worry about it." His hand gently rested on the small of her back. "I mean it. Just relax. I'm not worried about messy."

His smile was a little reassuring. Taking a deep breath, Cora unlocked the door and gently pushed it open. Dylan didn't wait for an invite – or maybe opening the door like that was the invite – and he walked straight in. Pausing in the middle of her one-bedroom apartment, he slowing turned in the middle of the room, taking in the open floor plan that was her kitchen, living room, and junk corner. Cora shut the door behind her and went to kick off her shoes.

"I told you that it was messy."

All he did was give himself one small laugh and shake his head. That was all Cora saw because in the next moment, his lips were on hers and her back was against the door.

She felt herself getting lost in everything. There was the taste of wine on his lips, on his tongue as it slipped into her mouth. His hands were on her sides, touching her face, grabbing her boob. His hips had her pinned, then moved against her and then stopped again. She felt warm all over and like her mind was a million miles away in the clouds.

Her hands had stayed at her sides, at first. The kiss had caught her off guard and she froze, caught up in the moment. Then they moved to Dylan's hips, feeling as he rocked against her. Her hands moved up and around his neck as the kisses got more demanding and passionate.

His hand ran up along her back and tugged down the zipper of her dress. The strapless floral thing fell to the ground when he took a step back. It was enough to break apart their lips and let Cora take a breath for the first time. Her eyes stared at him, half opened. His eyes were running over her body, devouring the sight of her.

"Dylan?" She wanted to ask what he was looking at but felt the air brush against her skin. She wanted to ask what was happening but couldn't get the words out.

There was a slight metal sound and, glancing down, Cora saw that he had unzipped his pants and heard his belt hit the floor. The bulge was evident in his boxer briefs, and Cora couldn't help but stare.

"Don't worry, babe. I got you tonight."

He reached around her head and pulled her face against his. While he drowned her again in the wine of his mouth, Dylan reached for her hand. He led her fingers to his waistline and brought her hand inside his boxer briefs. With his hand surrounding hers, he urged Cora to give his balls a little squeeze and then to wrap around his shaft. He guided her a few times along his throbbing self before slipping that hand under the cup of her bra and freeing her boobs.

Cora tried to stop, now that his hand had let her go, but he rocked his hips against her. He groaned as his skin still brushed against hers.

"Don't stop, babe," he whispered against her mouth.

Chapter Seven

Three red numbers glowed at her in the semi-dark bedroom. Cora hadn't been able to sleep at all. She knew exactly when Dylan had slipped out. It was ten minutes after midnight. The bed had rocked slightly as he rolled over and sat up. Cora had closed her eyes and pretended to be asleep, but she had watched the silhouette of his back for a moment. In her mind, she pictured Dylan glancing back over his shoulder to see if she was awake or not as he debated what he was doing. Maybe he could have even looked a little reluctant to leave her. He probably watched her with a hundred thoughts running through his head. One thing was for sure – he didn't see her as being a part in this relationship. What kind of guy would sleep with his girlfriend – for the first time – and then slip out like it was some one-night stand?

Dylan had eased out of the bed and fumbled around a little as he gathered up his clothes from their frenzied night. And still Cora didn't give him any clue that she was awake. His belt jingled a little as it slipped through the loops of his khakis. The only sound Cora heard between his pants going on and his escape to her front door was a single quiet squeak from the floor right next to her bed. There was one floorboard that was a little loose just outside the bedroom door.

The front door made the tiniest of clicks as Dylan shut it behind himself, but it was enough of a sound for Cora to hear, or to at least feel deep inside her chest. He had slipped away in the middle of the night as if she meant nothing to him. Maybe the worst part was that she had let him. So much could be said about him, but there was fault with her too. Did she really think so little of herself to be okay with this? Cora had let them have sex and hadn't spoken up. Before last night, Cora would have thought that they had a golden and unbreakable relationship. She would have sworn on the lives of all her credit cards that Dylan would have respected and understood her desire not to have sex. Her rectangular plastic companions' credit lives were now at the mercy of her scissors and the strength of her hand muscles that would cut them in half.

One of the tear-blurred red numbers changed.

6:49 AM

Cora pushed herself up and sat on the edge of the bed. Her legs dangled off the edge. She felt nothing but self-loathing and disgust. She had never felt lower or worse than she did right now. It wasn't the sex part even. Cora had done it before without feeling so disgusted and depressed afterwards. It was Dylan, and it was too late to realize that he'd make her feel this way. Maybe it was the wrong time or maybe he just was the wrong guy. She hadn't seen how wrong things were when the alarm bells were going off in her head, she brushed them away. She should have just walked away that day in the grocery store.

This was all her fault.

She couldn't stand herself right now. Cora felt just as dirty and disgusting on the outside as she did on the inside. There wasn't anything that she could do to scrub clean her inside. There wasn't anything she could do about the thoughts and her emotions. At least she had one shred of hope at sanity – she could scrub off all traces of any touch from Dylan from her body. She'd rub her skin raw or down to the bone, if she had to. That way, he'd be completely gone.

Cora forced herself out of bed and down the hallway to her bathroom. She turned on the shower, cranked up the hot water, and watched the steam cover the mirror. The hotter, the better. Dylan's touch needed to be burned from her body's memory. Her skin would be left raw and aching, but it seemed like a fair and just punishment for the sins she committed last night. She deserved to hurt. The strawberry crème body wash posted in the shower seemed too glamorous and rich and so far above what she deserved, even though it was from the cheap bargain bin.

The water pelted her the moment that she stepped into the shower. After forty-minutes, Cora's skin was rubbed raw and her soul felt burned, but the self-loathing and self-disgust remained. She just couldn't shake it this time and Cora didn't know why. Maybe it was because at every turn, she had convinced herself that Dylan was something more than what he was and that every single flaw and annoying trait of his was just an off moment. There were red flags all over the place and she purposely silenced the alarm bells going off in her head every time. And why? Cora had known from the beginning that Dylan wasn't worth her time, or rather that she wasn't worth his. They were not similar and, if you took away his looks, there was nothing about him that would grant him another breath or glance from Cora. She should have washed off his phone number before it ever reached her phone.

She grabbed a bath towel out from under the sink, where everything got stored. The fuzzy grapefruit pink towel wrapped around her body and tucked into itself to keep from falling straight down to the floor while Cora attempted to dry her hair. There were tangles from last night's mattress mambo and no amount of hair conditioner was going to set the locks of hair straight. Cora winced as she tried to pull through her comb on the first attempt. She got about a third of the way from her scalp when it came to a dead stop.

Cora screamed and flung the stupid comb across the room. It hit the wall and clattered down to the bathroom's faux tile flooring. Cora crumbled to the floor along with it. It wasn't the stupid comb or even her tangled hair. It wasn't even about Dylan anymore, and maybe it never was. She had let herself down. It was just that last night... It was a long time coming and it finally all caught up to her. Cora was someone that she didn't recognize anymore, and that frustrated and scared her more than anything.

On the floor, she curled up in her towel and let the pain seep out.

She was a stranger.

Every ounce of her being ached after spending hours on the cold bathroom floor. All the steam had dissipated, and the warm bath towel was gone, abandoning her at her lowest point to dry itself on the bathroom hook. Cora pushed her body up and off the floor. Slowly, she found her way back to her bedroom, stopping in front of the closet. It seemed almost ironic. Cora was so open about everything in her life except for how she felt about the future that she was told to have – specifically the familial expectations to get married as soon as possible and to have three kids before she was thirty. She hadn't thought that it was a big part of who she was, even if she chose to ignore it all. Cora was wrong whether or not she thought that was part of her, it was. The husband, the kids, the sex to make the kids...

She grabbed a pair of jeans, sliding them on one leg at a time. A pair of pants didn't make a whole lot of a difference, other that it felt like she was more covered and more protected from everything. It wasn't a long flowing skirt from a handcraft spouting merchant down the street, and it definitely wasn't a hundred different tie-dye patchwork garment that her sister wore. It wasn't something that Abuela Mariza would condone. And there had been a time where what Cora wore was accepted. Once upon a time, she trailed after her abuela and gladly played dress-up in the festive clothing, happily donning her heritage. There was a time when she liked someone telling her what to wear.

There was also a time where she loved being a beautiful and strong spirited Latina woman. She hadn't needed anyone to tell her that she was beautiful and smart and sexy. Cora had just known. And somewhere along the road, she had let that change. She couldn't see that strong and confident was beautiful. She couldn't see that she could be Latina and still wear what she wanted – where it was colorful or ethnic or not. Her exes had called her stubborn. Her family said she was ashamed.

But it was that, not at all.

Cora really wasn't stubborn nor was she ashamed. She just believed the people that were around her – the people that said that they loved her. It took most of her life, up until now, to realize it. She didn't need to pick one or the other.

But now there was the issue of her clothes. There were some that had too much of a sexy Latin flare. Cora had never really seen anything wrong with them before when she was growing up, but back then she really didn't have anything to show off. As she grew up and filled out, boys started to take notice of her. Even with her last ex-boyfriend, he had the image of her being some sex goddess or some passionate Latina lover. She hadn't tried to give Dylan any of those ideas, but he still had them. Looking at her closet now, maybe it was the clothes' fault. Clothes could sometimes make the man – or rather, the woman. People chose to see her a certain way. She pulled anything that showed an inch of skin or was tight out of her closet and tossed them on the floor in the corner. There needed to be a change in her life.

Cora grabbed a long-sleeved black and red flannel shirt to pull over the black camisole that seemed to be holding all the pieces of her together. The flannel was an old favorite and the most comfortable thing that she owned. Clothes didn't mean anything when you were able to speak and put your thoughts out there, but they could hide you away and give people a message to leave you alone. Cora had been struggling to speak up lately and be the real her. Maybe it would be better – or easier – to let her clothing speak for her for a while. Well, at least until she found herself or felt normal again.

Normally, she'd do her hair and make-up next. What was the point of going through that whole chore anyways? It was just to look pretty for the boys. Cora had though that it had been because it made her feel confident, like a bit of lipstick was her war paint. She didn't know if she could put on such a brave face anymore. She wasn't going to bother taming her hair either. Her Hispanic roots gave it enough of a curly that she could hide behind the waterfall of hair if she wanted. Anything to hide more.

Maybe tomorrow, she could pull her hair up into a ponytail and slap on some eyeliner. It was terrifying to think about looking in the mirror and not knowing what was going to be looking back at her. There were things that she wasn't ready to face, and maybe would never be ready. Today, Cora just wanted to curl up in the fetal position and protect herself. Nothing was going to change today, but maybe tomorrow everything would hurt less.

When her stomach growled, Cora couldn't remember when she ate last. Probably because in order to remember meant that she had to think back through all the rough times between right now and then. It was probably safe to assume that it was that dinner, so something like twelve hours ago. Cora knew that she needed to eat something even if she didn't think she could stomach it. Passing out and starving herself wouldn't make her feel better or do any good. She just needed something small and simple to ensure that her blood sugar didn't drop through the floor moments before the rest of her did.

The cellophane bag shook out the last two slices of bread to drop into the toaster. She took out a butter knife and just waited. It felt like she had to wait for everything to be done and over with. The toast. The day. Her life. She stared at the digital clock on the microwave. Finally, the metal box threw up her breakfast. Like the toast, Cora jump too, having been shaken out of the peaceful void.

She grabbed them out of the toaster and dropped the hot slices onto the plate. Peanut butter or jam? Well, a glance into the fridge proved there was no jam. There was butter, but that seemed like a less healthy option if she was being honest and wanting to make her life better. Cora tried to reason that peanut butter was a protein thing and healthy. Really, it was just yummy and deliciously gooey when it melted a little. Thinking about it made her smile a little and get a warm feeling inside – the first one she felt all day. Peanut butter it was then. She slathered the bland bread with the goodness and instantly regretted the bite she took when a moan escaped her.

Dylan had stolen so much from her.

She couldn't even enjoy one of her favorite foods and have a little bit of comfort food because she enjoyed it too much. It was ruined by what a moan made her think about. Something that she loved, that made her feel awesome, and could pick up her spirits was ruined. It was just ruined now. What Dylan did wasn't just limited to sex or how she looked at herself now – it was more than that. It turned off her appetite and there was no way that she could force herself into doing on more thing. She dropped the bitten slice of toast back on the plate and abandoned it in the kitchen.

The bedroom was so far off-limits that it wasn't funny. The bathroom was just as traumatic. The kitchen was now on her shit list. That just left the living room, but the television would just maker her think of moments she shared with Dylan somehow. If that didn't get her, the news would probably drag her down.

Cora plopped down on the couch and dragged her laptop off the small table. The two seconds that it took to boot up longer than normal was enough to bother her today. She was starting to feel like today was pointless and she should just go to bed and sleep until tomorrow. She just couldn't let things go.

"What the hell is wrong with me?" She lamented. Luckily, in his day and age, there was Google.

*I don't feel like myself anymore what's wrong
why do I feel empty*

142

had sex and feel different, why?
Boyfriend had sex and snuck out what does it mean
Is everything my fault?
how can I feel better
Why does sex suck

She offloaded the past twelve hours into the search box and hit "Enter". In 0.54 seconds, there was over eight hundred million matches. All of them were silly quizzes or rants on forums were people lived to troll others. Cora scrolled through the first two pages before finding something different.

AVEN

Her mouse hovered over the link. It was vague in the way, but could apply to her and what she went through? Asexual? That was one word Cora didn't know. It probably was just another pointless search result in the massive sea of links that half a second could throw out. At the same time, it was probably less of a waste of time than clicking some homemade quiz link where all it did was make the creator feel better about themselves when they looked at the results of those who took the stupid thing.

"An asexual person is a person who does not experience sexual attraction."

And there it was. It was laid out right on the homepage for The Asexual Visibility and Education Network, or what she already knew as AVEN. It seemed harmless enough, but it had already hit one of the things bothering Cora.

Their "About" section claimed it was founded recent enough, but there was no way this was really some new fad or thing. It – this sexuality – was probably around a long time but only in secret. AVEN claimed to have only two goals and they weren't life-shattering – acceptance and discussion.

But this couldn't be Cora... right? It was like saying that she like pineapple and that made her Hawaiian. This thing with the sex and how Dylan made her feel didn't just make her asexual. She had sex with her ex-boyfriend and she actually really wanted to have sex with him sometimes. This asexual thing meant that she didn't experience that... which she had in the past. It didn't stop the tears that streaked down her cheeks as she read the overview. This wasn't something that had the power to make her life more miserable, and it wasn't something that would make everything perfect. The more that Cora read, the harder it was to stop the tears. She read through pages and pages of the website as the words blurred out into nothing but smudges on her screen.

Wiping off her face, Cora fell into the forums. Her gaze and mouse drifted right away to the "Welcome Lounge". Everyone in the huge forum was new to the site. Every link that she clicked on had a new story to be told. Some were lost and confused. Some were just happy to finally have found a place where there were others like them. Some just needed a friend. Cora just needed a friend. Before she knew it, she had created her own post in the forum and spilled the same story into her first post that Google had filtered through to deliver her here to this safe place.

Another wave of tears hit her as, almost instantly, a dozen posts were added to her thread in the forum. Every single one of them was welcoming. Every one of them had a kind word towards her. A couple had similar stories and they posted a cliff note version of it, even offering some words of advice for how to handle what she was going through right now and different ways that they had found that were helpful in healing themselves. Cora never felt so loved by anyone outside of her own family until now. And now there were at least a dozen people in this thread right now that loved her enough to share their lives, experiences, and words to help her. They didn't even know her, but they were already there for her.

Cora took a couple hours to go through the forums. Slowly, she was starting to feel better about herself. Everything that happened, it wasn't completely her fault. Last night, she could have stopped things before they escalated and that will forever be partially on her shoulders. But it wasn't all her fault. Dylan should have respected her more and asked if things were okay before shoving himself inside. She would have been able to tell him that she didn't want to have sex. It felt like he had pressured her into it, and maybe that was true. But at the end of the day, they had both consented. That was something that Cora needed to learn to accept and live with. Her feelings and guilt were so misplaced. Reading the pages about asexuality helped to heal years of pain and confusion that Cora didn't fully realize that she had been carrying around with her. It helped, but it didn't completely take it away.

She didn't realize that it was getting late in the afternoon until her cellphone rang and jarred her out of her thoughts and self-discovery. Cora set the laptop back on the coffee table and went to find her phone, pulling it from the charger in the kitchen. It was her mother. It was only the first call – of what might turn out to be hundreds of calls – but it was still her mother on the other end. For once, she didn't feel the full amount of annoyance or dread when she saw that pop up on her caller ID.

"Hey, mama."

"Hello, Coriara." It was evident in the slow deliverance of her words that her mother was just as surprised.

Cora waited for her to say why she was calling. There was always a reason for her family to call. There was never just a random time when they called to check in and ask how she was doing. Not since the first day that she moved out of the house and there was a brief news story on the television about dirty produce in one grocery store. Her mother, and then her sisters, had called to tell her about the news story and to make her promise them that she'd never go there to shop for lettuce or tomatoes for her cooking. The joke was on them when they assumed that she was going to be doing any kind of real cooking.

"Mama, did you have a reason for calling me?"

The woman on the other end cleared her throat. "Ah, yes, um... I did have a reason."

There was another pause and Cora couldn't help but wonder if she really did have this so-called reason. There was no way that her mother knew about anything going on in her life, let alone Dylan and what happened last

146

night. None of her family really knew anything about what was going on in her life at all.

"Abuela Mariza decided to come back yesterday from visiting her friend in New York. She was supposed to stay with us another week, but she needs to leave early to go back to Mexico tomorrow. There's a bad storm that will be coming and she wants to make sure that her geraniums are off the stairs and out of the weather. We're having a family dinner for her tonight and I wanted to tell you to be there.

"Abuela doesn't know when she'll be back again for a visit. She's been joking that all her friends are almost dead and that her family could start making the trips to Mexico instead. I guess they gave her trouble with her visa this time and she thinks that because she needs to leave early that the government will deny her next time," her mother rambled on.

It was ridiculous that her abuela was more worried about some plants. A plant's sole purpose was to be outside and grow. A plant needed rain and that was undoubtedly coming along with this storm. It was probably some silly superstition that cut family time short.

She had come to visit family and friends. While, yeah, it was a bummer that she left so soon to visit her friend in New York, but Cora hadn't been heartbroken. Her family had been the ones to make a big deal out of it. Her mother spent her whole life with Abuela Mariza, and her sisters just had more time with her than Cora did. Cora was the baby of the family.

Then again, there was no asking with her family – just telling her when and where. Cora would have usually fought and argued and claimed to be in a bad reception area to end the call and puzzle her technically-impaired mother for a few hours. Instead, she was just drained and didn't care anymore.

"Sure, mama. Would it be okay if I'm there around six o'clock?" Cora threw it out there as a question. She wanted to make sure that she could cut down the family interaction time while not missing out on the free home cooking. Last time, she had been volunteered to cook. Hopefully, with showing up later, her mother may give her a pass.

That really must have been so far out of the ordinary that, for a while, there was nothing but silence on the phone. Cora could hear voices in the background, asking if she was going to be there or not. It sounded like her abuela. Only then did her mother say anything and it was just an "uh, huh". It was the strangest phone call that she ever had with her family, but it felt like a start to getting back to who she was.

"Hey, I have to go but I'll be there, okay?" Another two-syllable response was all that she got before the call ended.

Cora stared at the phone in her hand. She may have felt alright with her decision to try to rebuild things with her family. She may have felt better knowing that she could identify as being asexual and could try to understand what she felt and what she went through was actually normal – for her. She may have started to come to terms with Dylan and last night... well, not really.

It was tempting to go back online and spend a few more hours on AVEN. Although, she did just promise her mother that she would be at the family dinner tonight. She had to at least make an effort and, last time, she thought that she had only been online for ten minutes. If Cora went back online, she'd get lost in time and end up letting her family down. She was already dressed in something that was acceptable to leave the house wearing. It felt like it had been years since she slept, so a nap felt like it would do wonders for her. Again, there was a chance that she could accidently skip out on the family dinner and disappoint them.

What Cora really needed to do was the same thing that started all this – grocery shop.

She already knew that there wasn't much for her to eat in the apartment. Dylan's dates and leftovers from the family dinner had saved her from the chore. There was no doubt that Cora could snag more leftovers tonight and make them stretch for a couple meals. But thinking about going over to her parents' home made her realize something – she actually did miss cooking, at least part of her did. Like, real cooking and not the quick-and-easy things that she'd been popping in the microwave and surviving on the last couple of years. Homemade. Slow-cooked. Drool worthy food. And being in the kitchen for more than two minutes and forty seconds had always been fun – and slightly dangerous.

What the hell...

It was definitely strange to be standing here. It was the same spot that Cora fell prey to a pretty face and a horrible pick-up line. Yet, the meat case was deserted and safe. The ground beef wasn't making jokes about grinding her. The chicken breasts weren't competing with hers.

Cora realized that her hands were shaking a little and her breathing was off. It felt like her heart was pounding in her ears. Any moment, something was going to happen. She wanted to see who was coming, but she didn't want to look up. What if it was Dylan? What if he was here now? Was it Dylan? Whoever it was had just walked on by. Her breathing slowed a little, but Cora still felt dread and the uneasy.

She needed to tell herself that he wasn't here. No one was here. No one was looking at her. No one was going to bother her. It was alright. Just take a deep breath in, and let it go. Deep breath in. Slowly, Cora felt her body relax. At least her hands weren't shaking anymore.

She picked up a packaged of chicken thighs and walked along the outside of the aisles. She could see the ramen about halfway down one aisle. Then there was the Goya and taco aisle that was tempting her to return to the coolers to pick up something to stuff tortillas. At least Cora was walking further away from the frozen food aisle that had sustained her life, thus far. Instead, she headed into the produce section to grab cilantro, a lime, and some peppers for the rice she'd have to try figuring out how to cook... again.

She got in line at the register with the small bounty in her arms. It still felt different this time, but also the same. Cora set the handful of flavorful ingredients on the conveyor belt. Dylan hadn't exactly left his mark here but, as the cashier rang everything up and packed it neatly into a plastic bag, there wasn't exactly a feeling of dread and shame. For the whole time that she was with Dylan, there wasn't anything she really needed. Cora handed over the debit card and didn't flinch. There was more than a couple hundred dollars in her bank account at the moment. It was a blessing to come out of the worst moment of her life.

There was one thing that she was going to get slack over for later – the store-bought guacamole – but she'd like to think that it was the thought that counted when it came to family dinner.

Cora made a quick stop back at her apartment to drop off the groceries that she didn't need. She quickly looked up the bus schedules and debated ditching, for a second. Realistically, that wasn't going to happen. Family dinner needed to happen so that she could try to rebuild things with her family so she just wasn't the black sheep anymore.

The bus picked her up and dropped her off only a couple blocks from both her apartment and her parents' house. Walking up, she saw all the cars parked outside. Xo and Tommy were there already, and she wondered if maybe she should have just asked them for a ride. Then again, her sister probably had got here early to help with the cooking and that was something that Cora had already negotiated out of with her mother.

Her cousins were kicking around soccer ball in the yard, so she had to dodge them to make it inside. The most voices were coming from the kitchen, and that's where almost all her family was.

"Hola." Cora walked in and set the bag on the counter. Four faces stopped and turned to face her. Her sisters were surprised to see her, and it looked like even her mother doubted that she would show up at all.

"What's that?"

Cora reached into the plastic bag and took out the tub. Setting it on the counter, she told them the obvious. "I brought guacamole."

"Um, okay," her sister, Xo, said slowly.

"I couldn't get here early enough to help with the cooking, so I thought I'd bring something for us to nibble on while dinner cooked."

Her abuela walked over and picked up the tub of store-bought guacamole. Cora felt sick. This was not going to be okay with abuela. She was going to get lectured on how she was bringing shame to the family because she couldn't make something as simple as guacamole.

"Estoy feliz de que estés aquí. Gracias, Coriara." *I'm happy you're here. Thank you, Coriara.*

That was the nicest thing that her abuela had said to her in a while. But then it was followed by the worst question Cora could have expected – *Where's your boyfriend?*

"He couldn't make it. He had to work tonight." She should have expected this, but she didn't feel like she'd ever be ready to talk about him now.

"Wasn't he working last time too?" Xo asked. Her sister wasn't making anything easier.

"Yea, 'cos that's what people do." There was an attitude in her tone. She was hoping that they'd all leave it at that.

"Coriara, you should just accept that he does not want you and find a real man. I have a friend who has a son your age. I can talk to her and make a date happen," her mother offered.

"Mom, I don't need you to set me up on a date. Dylan's not here because he's working, okay?"

"Did he admit to cheating on you last time when he was out of town?" Xo poked the bear with that question.

"He didn't cheat on me. He was legit out of town for work."

And Cora was done with this. Since they changed the conversation back to English, her abuela had a hard time keeping up with what was being said. It was only a matter of time before someone translated for her. Cora didn't want to be around when that happened. She left the kitchen, heading out to the yard where her father and the men were.

"Hey, Coriara."

She sat down next to him on the picnic table. "Hey, dad."

"You trying to hide out here," Tommy asked, and she nodded. "Did your boyfriend come too?"

Great. Now Tommy and her father were going to get on her case too. Honestly, she wondered why she even bothered to show up. Maybe it was too late to get back to how things used to be with her family.

153

"No, he's working," she answered.

Her brother-in-law nodded. "How's things going with you two? Did you manage to work in some of that Patriot trivia yet?"

"Oh, yea." She had completely forgot that the last time they spoke that Cora had been trying to get the inside scoop. "No, it really didn't come up on our last date."

"You seem sad, Coriara," her father commented.

She wanted to just brush it off, but wasn't sure that they'd let it go. Unlike her mother and sisters, her father and Tommy weren't blinded by gossip and actually paid more attention to her.

"I don't think things are going to last with us. I'm not sure he's all that I thought he was."

"Sounds like something happened." Tommy reached over and rubbed her back.

Cora shook her head. She didn't really want to get into it with them. They wouldn't understand. Besides, if she told them that they had sex, her father would go ballistic. He would be off, rambling in Spanish, and looking for a gun to go shoot Dylan. They wouldn't even be able to listen long enough to hear that what really was eating her was how she felt *after* the fact. Her father wouldn't be able to understand why she was upset. There was a chance that Tommy might understand, but the forums on AVEN put that pretty low.

She opened her mouth to say something, but her mother had stepped outside to call them all to dinner. Cora just closed her mouth and followed after everyone else. She was just going to try her best to be invisible at dinner. If that wasn't possible, then she'd have to figure

154

out how to direct the conversation away from her. Last time she had come to a family dinner was to celebrate Diego and some soccer game of his. Maybe she'd bring that up – soccer.

Cora got off the bus and headed inside to her apartment. She had managed not to cry on the bus ride home, but just barely. Her family just triggered a lot with Dylan. She unlocked her front door and went inside, flopping down on the futon. She tossed her cellphone on the coffee table and noticed her laptop right where she left it. She could always try to distract herself again by surfing the website and reading stories again. Cora sat up and pulled the laptop over towards her.

Chapter Eight

Cora sat down with her bowl of cereal for breakfast to surf AVEN, and now it was almost dinner time. There was just one thing that she felt was lacking, for her, on the site – community. It was one thing to post on a forum where everyone could see your post, and where lurkers read instead of posting. She wanted – needed –a friend to talk to who'd understand.

Her "Welcome Lounge" post had been just that – people welcoming her to the site or to the asexual spectrum, but that was it. She didn't gain any friends from that. She debated joining the "Coming Out" forum but hesitated. It wasn't just the fact that her family wouldn't understand. She just simply wasn't ready to tell them, and she didn't know if she would ever even need to tell them. So, joining in on that forum was more about gaining attention than anything, and there had to be a better way to find a friend than that.

Besides, she would never need to "come out" to anyone except to her boyfriend. Right now, that may or may not be Dylan. She hadn't thought about him other than what happened that night, and now Cora really didn't know what to call him. Was he her boyfriend or just someone that she had dated? If she really was asexual, maybe all the bad stuff was in her head and she was just overreacting to it. Maybe it would be different if they had sex again and went slower, for her. Part of her didn't want to rule Dylan out of her future, but she was afraid of what he could do to her next. She felt empty and hated herself. Could that get worse? Would he try to help her feel better?

She wasn't sure that she wanted to tell Dylan anything at all. It was clear that he loved sex and she wasn't so sure how she really felt about it anymore. There had been a time in her life when she wanted it, and now there was a time when it felt like it had destroyed her. It wasn't like she could blame Dylan for wanting to have sex.

On the forums, it seemed like everyone knew who they were. Cora couldn't help but feel like she was the only one struggling as she surfed through the other forums and threads. Could she really be the only one feeling lost and hurting like this? It seemed like people were posting more about how to handle certain situations and which LGBQ events they were going to be crashing.

Then she found the right thread. A guy was talking about the pressure to have sex and, after doing it, the crushing feeling of self-disgust. There were some things that he said which Cora couldn't relate to, but most of it was mirroring her feelings – especially how it felt like he had lost himself and became a stranger to who he thought he was. Cora couldn't say that she was the same person after sleeping with Dylan, and she couldn't explain what was lost or different either. His post nailed it. There was that maddening feeling that couldn't be explained but it made you feel like another person was trapped inside your body, almost like they were poisoning you.

Cora didn't find many comments on his post that were helpful. It was just people saying that feeling will pass and not to force yourself to do anything you're not comfortable with. That was the issue though! They had done something they weren't comfortable with and needed to know how to heal from it, or even what was wrong with them now so they could fix it. Some commenters were in relationships with people that were normal and liked to have sex. No matter how much two people loved each other, if you suddenly stopped having sex, it would break your relationship. Some people might not really have a choice. Just like everything else – some things were easier said than done.

One person claimed that the only way to avoid this was to date another asexual person. Cora knew that she'd be looking for a needle in a haystack in a department store on Black Friday. She had a hard enough time as it was to date, and that was including every straight man out there. Asexuality was something completely new to her ears. So, what were the odds that there were any asexual men in Boston?

But the comment section seemed to think that such a place did exist. If Cora wanted to befriend and date other asexual people, then she had to go to the only place that really existed for that – Acebook.

Cora opened a new tab in her internet browser and typed in the website address. A very basic website page popped up. It almost didn't look legit. It looked like some high school web design class project. And "Acebook"? Yea, it was kind of a funny play on another big networking site. She stared at the simple homepage for a long time, debating whether or not to create a profile. It looked like it was another forum site. It would be a letdown if it was the same thing, different website.

Was it even worth trying?

But, honestly, what did she have to lose? Cora wanted a friend, if nothing else. She wanted someone to talk to that knew what she was going through and how she felt. After hours on AVEN, the person Cora was looking for was definitely not there. What was wasting a few more hours on Acebook going to hurt? There could be different people here and maybe she'd get lucky. It was worth the risk of wasting her time then.

She signed up for an account and filled out the few personal details that the website asked for. There was the option to upload a photo, and this was really where she froze. What if someone she knew saw her? Her mouse hovered over the button that would prompt her to upload a photo. There was probably the option to upload something that wasn't her face. But what did she really have to hide? If this was really who she was, then why hide? It's not like she was a lesbian or bisexual and people could openly judge her based just on who she held hands with or kissed in the street. As an asexual, no one would be able to tell from her heterosexual relationship. And if someone did find her on this website? Well, guess that meant that they were asexual too and shared that secret. And it would be a secret because no one had ever told her they were asexual.

A window popped up on the screen and asked where the photo she wanted to upload was located on her computer. Cora had a folder of photos – of herself – but she wasn't sure that she'd find anything that she would like in there. They were all photos of the "old" Cora. They were the laughing and fun Cora. They were just... not her. She managed to find one where she was looking at the camera – smiling – and cropped the photo so no one could see that she had been wearing a skirt.

Her profile was done, so it was time to just sit back and wait. She went to grab some potato chips to munch on. Her stomach had rumbled, seeming as she didn't get to eat all that she had wanted at the family dinner. When they started bringing up Dylan and everything, it had turned off her appetite.

There were no messages. That shouldn't have been a surprise. It had only been a couple of minutes. She could always logout and check back later but, really, there was nothing else that she had to do tonight. She had already explored every thread and forum on AVEN. Why not kill that time on this new website?

The first stop was Acebook's welcome thread where she could introduce herself. There were hundreds of pages of introduction posts, but the last new one was from three days ago. Cora took a deep sigh. She hoped that this place wasn't as dead as it appeared. She kept her post short and simple like the rest – when she discovered she was asexual, what she did for fun, what

161

she was looking for. Unlike AVEN, there were no sad stories and hurting people posting left and right. Then again, that wasn't supposed to be what this site was about. It was supposed to be a forum-style version of Facebook.

It was a little awkward to navigate, but Cora managed to pop into another forum. There were threads for "fun" ice-breaker games where you took the next letter of the alphabet and posted a photo of an animal that started with that letter. It was on the letter Z, so Cora quickly found a photo of a zebra online and posted it before anyone else could take the glory.

The next stop was, of course, the dating forum. AVEN didn't really have one just dedicated to finding someone. Theirs was more about posting and asking for advice or how to cope with your sexual partner. Acebook had that too, but there were actually threads where you could attempt to talk to someone and led things into a relationship. It did feel too soon for that. Besides, Cora didn't know if she was in a relationship or not right now, and she didn't want to call Dylan to find out. She just read over the posts, seeing who was out there and thinking about what kind of person they'd be in real life.

hey U up?

A message from Dylan popped up on her lock screen. She wondered if he knew what Cora was doing and what she was thinking – or rather, that she had just thought of him. It was a little creepy. Then again, maybe they really were just that much in-tune with each other.

wanna CU

She stared at the second message flash on her phone, which was sitting on the coffee table next to the computer. Cora tired to tell herself that they were innocent texts, but each one got her heart racing more. Why would he want to know if she was awake? It was almost eleven o'clock. If she was awake, why did he want to see her? There wasn't anything they could do this late. Restaurants were closed. It was too late to grab a movie. There were just bars open and Cora hadn't shown him that she drank much. She wanted the texts to be innocent, but she couldn't shake the thought that maybe she was wrong.

hey

One little text couldn't hurt... right? There was the chance that maybe Dylan meant that he wanted to see her, like as on a date tomorrow.

miss U
Can I cum there? Can be there in 10

He missed her? Cora stared at the phone in her hands. He said that he missed her. Maybe her heart was racing because she felt that connection and knew that what happened was just in her head – that she was the only making the other night a terrible memory. She didn't think much about the last text because he never spelled well and autocorrect always changed words to the weirdest things. Cora was halfway through typing a reply when a photo popped up in their chat.

She turned off the phone and set it back on the coffee table.

want U dis bad
let me pound ur pussy agin
I fuck u good babe

Cora flipped over the phone, so she didn't see the messages flash on the lock screen. It killed her to see those messages. They weren't from a loving boyfriend wanting to see her or from a guy wanting to take her out on a date. That was straight-up booty call material that Clarice always talked about. Dylan wanted her, but he only wanted one thing. He wanted the one thing that Cora now knew that she never wanted to give him again.

feeling sick

She caved and set one last text message before completely shutting off her phone. She didn't want to know if he messaged her back. There was either going to be a text wishing her well or one where he just didn't care. Both would hurt to read, but the latter would break the last shred of hope that Dylan might be a good guy. The latter text would make her realize that all that she was feeling wasn't just in her head and that it really was Dylan's fault for where she was now.

Cora was just done. She left everything on the coffee table and got up to head towards the bedroom. She didn't even bother to take off her clothes. They were more of a comfort to her now than they had been before, and she didn't want to risk seeing her body. Not even herself. Dylan had started to bring up things that she wanted to avoid. So, Cora climbed under the blanket on her bed and fell asleep.

Today, she was going to have to face the outside world. There was no way to avoid her shift today at work, and Cora wasn't so sure that she wanted to bail on what could be a great distraction. She could just zone out at her register and not deal with anything going on in her life right now.

Although, she didn't really have much time to think about herself this morning. Her phone had been left on the coffee table last night. It was shut off and it was usually used as her alarm clock. It was out of sheer luck that Cora got up. Unfortunately, that left only two hours to shower, get dressed, and make it to the store in time for her shift. It might be another Uber type of day.

Cora hurried through her morning the fastest that she could, which was hard considering that she took extra steps to avoid looking at her body when she showered and dressed. A pair of jeans and a dark Henley shirt were the things that she felt comfortable and safe in today. Her hair was simply pulled back into a ponytail and all the make-up that was on her face was a couple flicks of eyeliner. Having decided on just forking over the money for an Uber would leave her enough time to grab something to eat for breakfast. Seeing as she snuck out of the family dinner as soon as her mother and sisters started to take away the plates, Cora had returned without leftovers. Not that she would want to have a big meal like that for breakfast. Because she had braved the grocery store once, she had a few of the essentials. Which basically meant that it was cereal for breakfast and probably raiding the vending machine at work for lunch.

Sitting on the futon, it was unavoidable to see her laptop and phone taunting her. She was going to have to use her phone to get the Uber at some point. That was the most offensive of the two bits of technology, but the laptop was more dangerous. Every time that Cora went on it lately, five minutes turned into five hours. But what was more tempting was knowing if someone messaged her on Acebook yet or not.

She booted up the computer and waited for the internet to get her to the website. Between mouthfuls, Cora typed in her username and password. The website let her in and, at first, she didn't see anything. Then she noticed it – there were two messages waiting in her inbox for her. The first one was what seemed like a generic welcome message. The second, though, was from a real person.

TacoKing86:

Hey, LaFashionista! My name is Zach. You seem pretty cool and your favorite movie is one of my favorites too! Your profile said that you just found out you're asexual. It's rough in the beginning but it does get better. I've been out for almost ten years now. If you want a friend or just someone to talk to, hit me up. I'm usually always around.

Cora couldn't believe it. It was a legit message from a guy, and he wasn't trying to hit on her. Then again, that's probably not what asexuals did. They probably didn't use stupid pick-up lines. Besides, this guy messaged her and was trying to be her friend, which was what she wanted. There was no reason to ignore him then. But first, she had to check out his profile and see what this guy was really about.

The first things that she noticed, of course, was his profile photo. He had nice blue eyes that had an innocent look to them, which matched a nice smile. He had darker hair and he looked tall. Scrolling down the page, she found out that he lived in the United States and was a couple years older than her. He liked classical and rock music, and his favorite movie was *Pride & Prejudice*. That really surprised her. She wondered why he like that movie. Zach had heterosexual listed as his orientation, so it wasn't because he got hot and bothered over Mr. Darcy. It looked like his favorite food was Taco Bell – anything – and he was a dog lover but didn't hate on anyone with cats.

LaFashionista:

Hola, Zach. I'm Cora. Yea, I can't really believe you like P&P too. That's crazy. Are you gonna tell me that you can be my Mr. Darcy 'cos you kinda look like him and know how to sweep a girl off her feet?

In hindsight, the message that she sent Zach did come off a little harsh. It was probably just that her guard was up, and she knew that she was about to face the possible shitstorm of text messages from Dylan when she turned on her phone. Then again, she could just book the Uber through her computer. That was one way to avoid Dylan and his texts a while longer, so she did that and then hurried outside when the website warned her that the car would arrive in three minutes.

The driver dropped her off with barely anytime to spare. Cora hurried inside to punch-in before the clock said she was late. She didn't need to get lectured about tardiness at work right now. It might be the straw that broke the camel's back. She hurried pass the couple Plastics that were loitering in the breakroom.

"What a mess," one commented.

The other scoffed. "The walk of shame drab. Gawd, imagine the *thing* that would touch her. Gag."

Her feet got caught up for a second and almost made her trip and fall. That would have made things a hundred times worse. It was bad enough that she got noticed and worse that they were poking fun at her clothes. Her clothes were supposed to be her protection from the world. They were to cover her and make her feel comfortable, not make it seem like she woke up and ran out of a one-night stand.

It got to her.

Cora tried to avoid the customers milling about in the store and went straight to her register. She didn't turn on her light right away, which confused a few people who were waiting to check out. They eventually gave up and headed to one of the lines that another Plastic girl had open. Needless to say, it got her a death stare from the Plastic girl. No doubt that she was going to squeal to the boss and snitch on Cora. Taking a deep breath, she flicked on her register's light.

People kept lining up and it was a steady stream of customers. It seemed to go on for hours, days, years. But it also stopped Cora's mind from wandering and the repetition of swiping barcodes meant that she didn't need to think.

"Cora, go take your lunch."

She had to snap herself out of it and realize that the boss was standing in front of her. The boss must have turned off the register's light at some point because it was dark and there was no line of customers waiting to check out.

"Oh, um… okay."

Cora wasn't sure if she was hungry and, even if she was, she kind of wanted to avoid the lunchroom. She didn't want to end up around any of the Plastics. She just couldn't handle hearing their snide little comments today. Especially when they hit so close to home and brought up all the stuff that she was trying to forget. If she was going to avoid the lunchroom, she might as well find somewhere to chill outside and try calling her best friend. It had been too long since they talked and maybe she knew something about asexuality. If not, maybe Cora could "come out" to her and see what that was all about. Not a day in her life did she think that she'd have to do something like that. Not that she was forced to now, but

Cora felt like maybe she could let her best friend know how she was feeling.

She pulled out her cellphone once she got to one of the park benches that were along the sidewalk, a ways away from the store and those horrible Plastics who'd probably try to overhear her.

"Hey, guuuurl," Clarice picked up the phone.

"Hey... is this a good time?"

"Oh, shit. What's going on?"

Cora sighed. She could see why Clarice would think that. Usually when someone asks if you have time right away it means that they either have a long story to tell or they got some bad news.

"It's nothing like that." Best to set her at ease first and not have her best friend worrying over nothing. Well, for no major reason.

"Are you okay?"

She shook her head and then realized that Clarice couldn't see her. "No, not really."

"Okay, Cora, can you just tell me what's going on then?" There was a hint of annoyance in her friend's voice. "This got anything to do with that hottie you're seeing?"

"Not really, but kind of?" She knew that it wasn't all about Dylan. What Cora really wanted to talk about was the fact that she was probably asexual and seeing what Clarice would then say.

"Spill the details. You guys must be banging, right? I mean, with a dick like that it must be pretty fucking good. Tell me! Tell me!"

It seemed like talking about being asexual might have to wait or, at least, it was something that she'd have to build up to. "Fine, okay. Yes, we had sex once."

Clarice cheered. "I knew it! I knew there was no way that you couldn't try a dick like that. So, tell me how it was."

She wasn't sure that she wanted to talk about this anymore. It was making her think more and more about what had happened, and then about the way that it had made her feel afterwards. But Clarice was so into knowing the details, and she wanted to kind of make her friend happy.

"Well, you know, it just kind of happened. He came over. We did it. He left."

"So, he sucked?" There was the sound of utter disbelief in her best friend's voice. As if a guy like Dylan could ever disappoint. "Gawd, I hate minute men. We can find you someone better than that."

Cora's brain was just gone, and she couldn't catch the thought before it got out. For some reason, she felt the urge to defend him. "He didn't last a minute."

"Oh? Oh... he came before that? Wow, pathetic. To-tal loser."

"He was fine." She needed to get her friend off the subject of Dylan and onto the subject that she had originally wanted to talk about. "I don't want to talk about him, though. That's not why I call you."

"Okay, fine." Clarice sighed. She clearly was disappointed that she wasn't going to be getting any more details. "So what did you want to talk about?"

"Have you ever heard of asexual before?" Cora told herself not to start rambling. She just needed to know if Clarice had heard of it before or not. If Clarice had, then she needed to know what she thought before Cora could decide on coming out to her or not.

"Hmm… no, don't think I ever have. What is it? Is that why you don't want to talk about the hottie?" He has this asexual thing?"

Clarice really had no idea what asexuality was. She probably thought that it was something like herpes or a medical problem that a certain blue pill could fix. It would have been easy for Cora to let her think this and just drop the conversation. It wouldn't change what Cora was or how she felt. Then there was the chance of the scenario with Dylan happening again the future – whether with the real Dylan or with another guy like him.

"There's nothing wrong with being asexual. Some people just are," Cora started.

"O-kay." It didn't sound like Clarice was buying it.

Maybe this was going to be too hard. Cora was still trying to accept this herself, after all. "Well, let me ask this then. Is there something wrong with being gay?"

"Uh, no… wait." She seemed to have figured something out. "Is Dylan gay or are you coming onto to me? Like, Cora, I'd be flattered but we're best gals and I love dick way too much."

"No one's gay, Clarice. I'm just trying to… ugh. Okay, so, being asexual is just like being gay but in the way that you're sort of like something different than everybody else." Well, except that – in this case – you just don't like anything.

Clarice was quiet for a long while. "Different like how? Like you're into furries or some imaginary stuff?"

"More like you don't like sex at all," she tried to say but it ended up sounding more like a question.

"Are you asking me 'cos you don't know? Because if he told you that, Cora, then run because it sounds like some bullshit to me."

She couldn't handle the rollercoaster of emotions when it seemed like Clarice was close to figuring it out only to throw a curveball out the window. "I'm asexual, Clarice."

"Wait, what?" Clarice stuttered.

"I'm asexual," she tried to sound more sure of herself this time.

Clarice didn't know what to say then said the one thing she could think of – deny it and get Cora to change her mind. "No, you're not. You just said that you and the hottie banged. Plus you and your ex were always hooking up. You lost your virginity to him."

Clarice wasn't wrong. She did have sex with her ex-boyfriend, but something just seemed different back then. Maybe she wasn't completely asexual then or maybe it was just that they had a deeper connection than her and Dylan did. Cora had sort of read about the different types of asexuals on AVEN but it had been late and, honestly, just confused her more.

"Having sex doesn't mean that I'm not asexual," Cora defended herself.

"But doesn't it, though? Plus, you even liked it with your ex," her best friend pointed out.

Cora didn't have an argument for that. She shrugged it off. "Guess things changed."

"Did they really change or was the hottie just that awful and you don't want to admit it?"

She knew that Clarice was probably just trying to figure out if this guy was sticking around or not, and then probably why Cora had made up such a crazy story. It was obvious that Cora wasn't acting like herself. Her friend's biggest fear was probably that she was using this asexual thing to cover up something worse like Dylan had beat her or forced her into some weird shit.

"I changed, Clarice. Yea, I liked sex with my ex-boyfriend. Sex with Dylan was okay and he was okay, but it just didn't feel right. And then I went online and found this place where everyone feels the way that I do. Like, I can say that Dylan's hot but it's not like I'm thinking about wanting sex from him when we were doing it." It was all starting to ramble out. "I mean, he didn't force me into it but, like, there was this pressure to just let him do it. I wasn't really into it but it seemed like he was and I didn't want to make things bad. Then he left right after, so it was all just like –"

"He's an asshole," Clarice cut her off. "Let's never talk about him again, okay? He's a dickhead and so not worth your breath. You deserve so much better than that."

Cora wasn't sure what to say, but it felt like maybe her friend finally got it. Now she wished that she had done this in person so that she could get a hug, because she

174

could really use one right now. She was all emotional and just wanted to cry it all out again.

"Thanks, Clarice. I... I really mean that." And Cora did. "Listen, I have to get back to work. I'm on my lunch and the Plastics have it out for me."

"Okay, yea. Call me anytime ya need, okay?"

"Okay." She hung up the phone. Talking to her best friend – and even coming out – had made her feel better. Maybe she could do this. Maybe it really was okay to be her, even if being her meant that she was asexual.

Taking a deep breath, Cora tried to calm herself before getting up and walking back to the store. Just a few more hours and she could get away from all those toxic girls and all these stupid customers. She'd be able to go home, maybe eat some ice cream, and binge watch something on Netflix. Everything could get better.

There was a message from Zach waiting for her when she got back from work. The frustrations of the day – between the Plastics and then the phone call with Clarice – disappeared a little. It looked like he really was an actual person that might want to be her friend. After the thing with Dylan, she knew not to get her hopes up, but it was really hard. Cora found someone like her and someone that offered to be a friend – even when she was kind of mean in her message back.

TacoKing86:
I swear that I want to just be friends. I'm demisexual, so I don't go after someone until I have a strong connection

with them. Not trying to say that I'm trying to do that with you. I can have friends that are just friends.

Being completely honest, I am single right now. I'm not really looking for anything, but I won't pass up any chance that comes my way. I live in Chicago. City boy born and raised. Are you from Boston or the suburbs? And please tell me you're not a Patriots fan :P

This meant that she had a chance to turn things around and to at least apologize. Her whole goal had been to make a friend. If this guy was still willing to talk to her after her attitude, then it would be crazy to throw that away. He obviously knew shit happened and maybe that she took it out, wrongly, on him.

LaFashionista:

Hey, sorry about my last message. I was seeing this guy and things just got bad. Like he's the reason that I'm asexual. And, no. Not a Patriots fan. I don't really like sports. To answer your other question, I'm from Boston. City girl born and raised here ;) So, Chicago... what's that like?

Cora hoped that he'd send her a reply. She really didn't want to go looking and to have to try to make friends herself. The idea of messaging people only to be ignored was a rejection that she couldn't handle right now. On the flip side, there was the rejection of never getting a message like Zach's from anyone else, or one back at all. Right now, she needed making friends to just be easy.

TacoKing86:

Hey, I get it. I figured you might just be figuring things out 'cos your profile is a little bare. Then I saw your post in the newbie thread. Sorry that guy was a douche. I'm here if you wanna talk about it. And I don't think he's the reason you're asexual, but he might be why you know now. Sometimes we've got to believe that God made up this way for a reason. That's why we all must have faith that we'll find the one we need. Whether that's a friend or a significant other. So, don't give up hope that you'll find what you're looking for too.

Also, Chicago is cold. Very cold. But the pizza here is great... and the beer too!

Zach had written back before she could log off. She hadn't noticed the tiny green dot at the corner of his profile photo, but she did now. Knowing that he was online made Cora nervous. Would he be waiting for a quick reply back too? If she tried to send a fast reply, there was a bigger chance that she'd end up looking stupid. And what if she sent a reply, he stayed online for a while, and then logged off without writing her back? Would that have meant that he had reached the point where he was fed up and ditching her?

LaFashionista:

I'll give ya the pizza, but do you really think Chicago beer is better? We got Samuel Adams and like a bunch of other stuff too... You said in your first message to me that you were demisexual. I tried figuring that out before, but it was just confusing. Is it too much to ask you to try and explain that? Can I still play the newbie card?

TacoKing86:

Sure. So, as a demisexual, I don't really experience all that "I need to get in their pants NOW" kind of thing. I also don't really think about sex at all, which everyone assumes as a guy that it's on my mind. Demisexuals, I've notice, need to have like a best friend or kind of end up really close to one or a few people. It's like that type of relationship is good enough and what we really want. People best describe it as "platonic". But when I get really close to someone, then it's like my mind almost lets me think of that person in more than one way. With my past relationships, they were all my friends for a couple years before we thought about dating. Like, if I don't really know someone then I can't even consider being attracted to them. Not everyone really understands this – both in the ace community and the rest of the world. Demisexuals are like halfway between "real" asexual and being horny fucks. Does that make any sense, or did I just make it more confusing?

LaFashionista:

No, I think I get it more now. Like, my ex-boyfriend and I had sex and it was fine, but with the last guy I was seeing it was the complete opposite. I felt forced the whole time and the wanted to vomit. Even days later! I went to my parents for a family dinner and it got me thinking about how I was feeling but in a way that maybe someone else could understand – I'm a taco. Like how is it that hard

178

shell tacos survive the factory, the delivery trucks, the stores, and then break as soon as you put something inside them?

There was a little bit of regret after Cora sent that message. She realized that she had started talking about sex. Every time sex had come up in the past, that's where the conversation stayed. This message might be the thing that put the nail in the coffin.

TacoKing86:
Well, it sounds like you may be demisexual like me. I don't want to assume your feelings or what you are. But definitely check out demisexual again. There's a thread where some demis posted to try and explain things.

Zach had included the link to the thread in his message. Clicking the link, it took her to a thread with over twenty pages and a disclaimer that this wasn't an all-inclusive list. This was an explanation about demisexuals by demisexuals and it was told through their experiences. It seemed like a lot of people were asking questions, and for each question at least three people chimed in to comment on it.

She ended up spending the rest of the night reading through the thread that Zach sent her.

Dylan had tried calling her last night, but she had ignored him. It was reasonable to assume that he would have left her a voicemail or at least a text message to call him back. That's what she would have done if she couldn't get through to someone. He had done neither of those things.

It wasn't like she was complaining though. It was a nice break not to be bombarded with flirty text messages or worrying about what was going to happen during their date. It gave her time to think about herself and look into demisexuals again like Zach had suggested. It made more sense the second time that she read over the definition and it really did help to read through that thread. It didn't hurt that Zach seemed to have been sticking around and willing to answer her questions. Cora didn't feel like she was going at this alone anymore.

LaFashionista:

I've been thinking about what you asked in your last email. About what I want for myself. You know, I still don't know 'cos it's like what I want hasn't really changed. I want to get married eventually and start a family. A normal family and not one like my crazy family. Like, I don't want to force my thoughts and stuff on my kids. Did you know that there's a list of approved baby names that I can call my kid? FYI Zach isn't on the list. Neither is any name that I would actually want to name my baby. And then I think about actually having kids and it terrifies me. Like, almost to the point where I just wanna adopt.

TacoKing86:

Is it because of the pain of labor or the fact you have to have sex with someone? If it's about the labor, then yea –

that shit's whack. But the sex part doesn't have to be so bad. You had said it yourself that there had been someone you enjoyed doing it with. You just got to find The One again. And Zach is an awesome name! Should I write your family a dissertation on "Zach" and try to convince them to change their minds and add it to the approved list?

LaFashionista:
They're stubborn Mexicans, so I doubt that you'll be able to change their mind. Thanks for offering though. So... how'd things go with that girl?

Cora didn't really want to ask him about the date that he went on, but she had to ask. She wanted to know if her friend would still be there to be... well, her friend. Okay, and part of her was hoping that at some point their friendship may become more. They talked every day, and sometimes more than she even talked with Clarice. Zach was interesting and seemed like a real good guy. There hadn't been a single time that she thought he was lying to her or that he was acting like an asshole. His "good guy" persona actually seemed legit, unlike Dylan's "good guy" act.

She hadn't told Zach that she really was identifying as demisexual too. Everything that he had said about himself and how he felt in the dating world was how Cora was feeling. Like, the more time that went on while she was talking to him, the more Cora found that she really liked him. Having only seen the photo on his Acebook profile, it wasn't like she was ready to drop her panties – as Clarice would put it – but she could honestly

181

say that she was attracted to Zach, and the thought of maybe having sex with him didn't seem so horrible. Although, Cora didn't know how he really felt about her. Maybe he didn't see her that way and never would see her as more than just a friend.

TacoKing86:

Turns out that we have nothing in common. I think that she was also looking for a polyamorous relationship too. I wouldn't be the sexual partner, but I'm not one to share the person I love and care about. Call me selfish or call me old fashion. So, you get any dates or are you still recovering from that asshole?

Dylan.

Yea, she still wasn't completely rid of him. He occupied less and less of her thoughts, but that just made her worry more. He knew where she lived and Cora wondered how long it would be before he came knocking on her door. And what would she do then?

He was still texting her. While the texts had dialed back on the explicit sexual nature, they still were too flirty for her and way too forward. Having been talking to Zach, she could see that Dylan's messages were more forceful. If she hadn't been talking to another guy, she might have just gone on thinking that this was how all men talked these days.

LaFashionista:

He's still texting me but I'm trying to ignore them. Been a week since the last dick pix, so yay!

She didn't know what else to say, so she just sent the message. Zach was online, so it wasn't like she could really go MIA and stop replying to of the blue. But now that she thought of dick pix, she couldn't help but wonder what Zach's would look like. It was completely out of the question to ask him to send her a photo, and it definitely would make things awkward if she asked him to describe his penis to her. It wasn't like she wanted that to be what led to anything happening between them, but it was a thought that wasn't easy to shake from her head. Like, it was irrational to want to know what his dick was like when she'd never see it and never touch it... and because they were just friends.

But Cora had already daydreamed about one day going on a date with him. The night always ended with him sitting on the couch with her, and she'd be snuggled into his side. That was all she had really wanted. And maybe that's where this nagging thought about what was in his pants was about – she wanted to fantasize about what sex might be like with him.

TacoKing86:
Good for you! Next time he bothers you, though, you should tell him off. Tell him that he can go put his dick in some other chick! Haha that rhymed :)

LaFashionista:

LMAO I should! You are awesome, Zach! But is that a thing all guys do? Like, do you send dick pix?

Cora knew that it was a giant leap to make from talking about Dylan to fishing for news about Zach's dick. It was probably something that she should be doing. Not only because Zach was a new friend, but also because he was asexual too. She didn't know what his limit was and what may trigger him. If she triggered him, he may ditch her and then it would all been for nothing. She wouldn't have a dick pix. She wouldn't have a chance to date him. She wouldn't have a friend at all, probably.

TacoKing86:
Are you trying to see my dick? Le gasp!

Oh, she messed up. She messed up big time. He caught her fishing to hints about what it looked like. Cora was so stupid. Why couldn't she have just let things go? Now she had probably ruined the best thing she had going for her and lost a really good friend too.

LaFashionista:
What? No. I mean, no. I'm sorry, Zach. Please don't stop being my friend. I really like you and I like talking to you. You're the first guy – well, first person – to really understand how I feel. I'm sorry. I'm just a fucking mess...

TacoKing86:
It's fine. I'm teasing ya, Cora. But you probably shouldn't be asking around about dicks. There's some

184

really weird people out there. And no, not all guys send dick pix. I'm one that doesn't. Never really saw the point in it. Either you're my friend or my lover. One doesn't need to see my dick, like ever.

TacoKing86:

You live in Boston... right? I may be taking a trip out that way. My little sis wants to see New York City before she goes off to college and my parents have been talking about making it this whole thing. From what I'm told, there's a train that goes between NYC and Boston. So, any interest in meeting up? I can promise that I won't whip out my dick, if you're thinking that I'm a horny guy after you tried to proposition me ;)

Cora knew that her face was a million shades of red right now from the level of embarrassment that she felt. It took her forever to gain the courage to peek up at the train wreck on her screen. That's when she saw his second message. It seemed like she hadn't scared him away, and that only made her wonder why. She was a hot mess on a good day – and today wasn't a good day.

It seemed like he had just laughed it off as nothing. But the part that worried her was that Zach brought up maybe meeting in person. Because he lived halfway across the country, she didn't think it was ever going to be possible to meet up. And the fact that he might be willing to come to Boston, as in where her crazy family live – which he knew about! – blew her mind. He must be crazy.

And yet, she felt a little excited over the idea. If he really was going to be coming out this way, then she had to meet him. The only thing was that Cora would have to save up money for the visit, just in case she needed to buy a train ticket to see him.

LaFashionista:

Boston is also where my crazy family is – just warning you! But yea, I'd love to meet up with you. Do you think your family would really be okay with you just running off or some Latina following you around?

TacoKing86:

My family's pretty chill, but I'll run it by them first. After all, I'm a big boy now and can do what I want – like have ice cream for breakfast :) But we should swap numbers so we can talk easier. Plus, we'll need some way to find each other when we meet up. Is that okay?

LaFashionista:

Yea, that's fine by me. Just letting you know that I do like funny animals and memes lol ;)

She sent that last message with her phone number. Cora hoped that their conversations just wouldn't end because they swapped phone numbers. That's why she had told him what she liked, hoping that he'd send her photos of funny animals or some really hilarious meme that he found.

It did make her worry that he would just disappear until his family came out on that trip to New York City –

186

whenever that was. It was probably irrational, but Cora had almost lost him once tonight with stupid talk.

Hey, baby. It's me. Wanna bang?
Okay, sorry, just kidding. It's Zach. I don't know why I thought it was a good idea to txt that
Please don't hate me 4 trying to be funny? I'm an idiot :)

Cora rolled her eyes. It was an opportunity to mess with her, and he took it. He just didn't do it so well. He hadn't even given her time to freak out or to think that Dylan was texting her from some random burner phone. Honestly, she could see that Zach had only been trying to joke around and play off what they'd been talking about.

I don't hate u... now send me memes :D

Afterward

Cora identifies with someone who is demisexual, on the asexual spectrum. For the first half of the book, there's nothing to tell us that she's anything but a "normal" woman in the dating world. She has emotions and thoughts just like anyone else. She can see someone as being attractive and even have strong feelings about them – sexual or otherwise. That's because there is absolutely nothing wrong with being asexual.

The way that Cora comes to find out that she's asexual is one of the many ways people realize this for themselves. Some people find out early in life that they're asexual, and others find out later in life – even after getting married and having children. Cora could have seen a photo of a nude man and realized that wasn't for her, and either known then that she was asexual or struggled with the idea that maybe she was just a lesbian. Everyone's story and experiences are different – even two people who identify the same way.

One question Cora ponders is why the sexual experience with Dylan was so vastly different than the sexual experiences she had with her ex-boyfriend. This leads her to believe that there was something wrong with her, personally, when it is easily explained by the definition of demisexual. With Dylan, he was mainly interested in no-strings-attached sex and afterwards was messaging Cora for hook-ups. She does mention that he was asking for a "date" but – from Dylan's perspective – it was just the bait to get her to agree to see him again and to give him an opportunity to push things to a sexual place. With her ex-boyfriend, and even Zach, there was an established relationship there and a foundation of friendship. These two men were not the fly-by-night types to come in one moment and disappear the next. Cora is able to feel a deeper connection with someone who is actually in her life, and that connection can lead to a sexual attraction and an intimate relationship.

It may seem like Cora has overcome her feelings of regret and disgust, but that's not necessarily true. Just like you can't tell by looking at someone if they're asexual or not, you can't look at someone and know what they are feeling. It is true that Cora has been able to avoid her triggers – which is Dylan and the sexual experience with him – but she is in a place where she can ignore, mute, and block his calls and messages. That's why it is a true fear for her that Dylan could just show up at her apartment. For the most part, the saying that "out of sight, out of mind" does hold true. Asexuals live normal lives and nothing changes until a sexual aspect comes into place. Even so, Cora now knows that sexual messages and images can trigger her and, even though she doesn't encounter them often, there's the knowledge in the back of her head. So, when her mind wanders, it may come up and trigger those feelings. It's not something that she's completely dealt with and overcome.

One thing that does not come up is how asexuals are treated in the LGBT+ community. While things are slowly changing, asexuals are not widely accepted or acknowledged. The argument is that the LGBT+ community is about sexual minorities and the fact that asexuals are the void of sexual preferences. The asexuals that do find acceptance tend to be individuals that also identify as homosexual or bisexual because the LGBT+ recognizes that part of their sexuality, even if is dismisses the asexual portion. Because of this, asexuals don't often find support in the LGBT+ community – where the "A" stands for "ally" instead of "asexual" – and feel alone and isolated. Advocates for asexuality and the work that AVEN does to bring awareness are helping to change this and create a safe, accepting place for asexuals and their allies.

For more information about asexuality, please visit the following websites:

The Asexual Visibility and Education Network:
www.asexuality.org
Acebook: *www.ace-book.net*

More to Come...

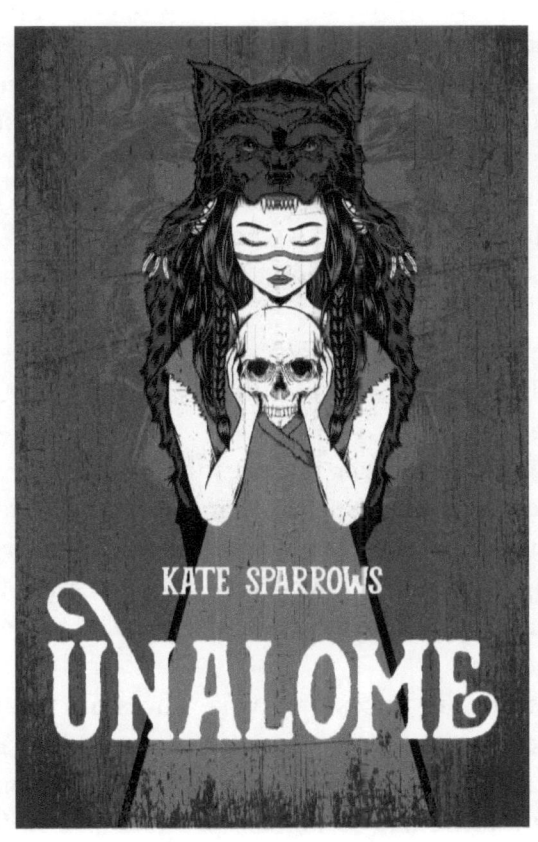

CHAPTER ONE

"No matter what, my little Eira, I must protect the hawthorn tree."

He motioned for me to come and sit on his knee as he sat on the large stone, in sight of the tree. I still can't understand why papa would rather sit out here in the grove surrounded by trees all day instead of be at home with me and with mama – who is pregnant.

"It's just a tree," I point out. "What makes it more special than me?"

Papa smiled and shook his head at my petulance. "This tree is our ancestors. It is sacred to the Unalome people."

That didn't answer my question. It didn't prove why the tree was more special than me and the new baby arriving. I wish someone would just burn that tree away or chop it up. All it did was take my papa away from me and put him in a scary place in the middle of woods filled with beasts.

"It's not our ancestors, papa. Ancestors are people." Just like my grandfather was. It's scary to know my papa is a killer. Because he is priest to the Unalome, that means that he had to kill the previous priest. My papa killed his father and, while I never really knew him, I can't help but be sad that someone in my family is gone.

"All of our important rites happen here, Eira. You will marry beneath this tree and you will be sent off into the next life below these branches as well. This tree bears witness to it all, and all the souls of our ancestors find peace being here." He pulls me into a hug. That must mean what he is about to say may upset me. "When it comes time for a new priest, my blood shall stain the soil and be absorbed into the hawthorn, just like every priest before me."

I can't stand the thought of someone hurting papa. His blood should stay right where it was – inside his warm body, so that he could always hold me. "But why do you have to die? If the tree needs blood, can't you just cut your hand for it?"

It may have sounded like a stupid question, but papa didn't hear it that way. I was just a small girl who loved her father. "That is the way it has always been and always will continue to be."

I tried to push myself off his lap, but he held me tight. I didn't want to hear him talking about dying and leaving. How could he say that when I was about to have a baby brother or baby sister? Mama needed him. The baby needed him. And I needed him. I needed to go find a way to keep papa safe forever.

"Eira, do you know what Unalome means?" He waited until I shook my head. "Unalome means "the journey to enlightenment". When written out, it is a symbol of many twists and turns that remind us that the path isn't always straight or perfect or even in the right direction. You are Unalome, as am I. We are all merely on a journey to enlightenment, and sometimes that means we may not understand the moments along the way and why they happen."

I'm sure that papa thought what he said was the answer that I needed to hear in order to make everything alright. It didn't make anything alright. It was enough, though, to make papa think that things were settled and to allow me to slide off his lap. I pretended that I needed to fix my plain linen dress when I was really waiting to hear what he wanted me to do. I knew that he would send me home now to look after mama and to help cook dinner, but I didn't want to go just yet. The woods did scare me because I knew what beasts roamed in there. But I didn't get much time with papa, and I wanted to stretch that out a little while longer.

"Hurry home now, Eira." He kissed the top of head then stood, walking back over to the hawthorn tree. "I will see you in the morning when you bring me a meal."

My shoulders hung. I didn't really want to leave now, but I could not disobey my papa. I didn't want to make the long walk home with my bottom stinging at every step. It meant that I would suffer the pain of my disobedience only for mama to understand what I had done and punish me as well. It was forbidden to disobey the priest, and it was punishable to disobey a parent or elder. I would be doing both and deserved all the pain that would come my way.

"Night, papa." I started to sulk off but stopped at the edge of the grove. "I love you."

"I love you too, my little one." There was that familiar sadness in his tender tone. I knew he did not like this anymore than we did. I just don't know why he ever made the choice to become priest and kill grandfather. I probably would never know.

Kate Sparrows

Kate Sparrows is a Sassy Sue.

She's a cynical hopeless romantic that's in love with her Kindle and book boyfriends. It's really a love that you shouldn't come between. Well, unless you have ice cream, an awesome accent, or an amazing book in your hand. Bonus points having for all three.

Acknowledgements

Anyone who has ever dated can attest that it's hard. First, you have to make yourself vulnerable. Then you have to decide to either wait or go searching for what you want. Then you'll have to talk to someone and hope that what you want matches what they want. Everyone knows that if you're gay or a lesbian that your global options are halved, and if you're bisexual that you double your chances. At the end of the day, chances are that everyone will engage in sexual activities... but what if what you're looking for isn't sex? Society puts a lot of pressure on the milestone of sex and our parents make comments about wanting to be grandparents. Asexuals have been fighting a silent fight. So - to anyone who's identified this way and been through this – you deserve to be seen and recognized. I'm sorry for what you may have been put through.

You will find what you're looking for.

Always stay true to who you are.